TEA[illegible]

"I think Mr. Bach—I mean Stuart, is going to be a wonderful teacher," Elizabeth said to her friends as they walked down the hall after their first painting workshop. "He so obviously cares about painting—and about us."

For a brief instant Olivia felt stricken. Did Stuart care about all of them equally? Had she imagined that he had singled her out? Or was there—was she completely wrong in hoping—a real connection between them?

"Olivia, you're awfully quiet today," Elizabeth said. "What did you think of the class?"

Olivia bit her lip. The next minute she blurted out, "I think Stuart Bachman is the most wonderful man I've ever met!"

Elizabeth and Enid stared at each other, obviously taken aback by the force of her outburst. Olivia blushed and added, "I mean, he's so dedicated. He seems like an excellent teacher."

But she could tell she had already given herself away. It wasn't surprising, either. Feeling the way she did, Olivia expected that in no time the whole world would know that she was in love with Stuart Bachman. Madly in love. She didn't know how she would endure the agony of waiting a full day until she could see him again.

Bantam Books in the Sweet Valley High Series
Ask your bookseller for the books you have missed

#1 DOUBLE LOVE
#2 SECRETS
#3 PLAYING WITH FIRE
#4 POWER PLAY
#5 ALL NIGHT LONG
#6 DANGEROUS LOVE
#7 DEAR SISTER
#8 HEARTBREAKER
#9 RACING HEARTS
#10 WRONG KIND OF GIRL
#11 TOO GOOD TO BE TRUE
#12 WHEN LOVE DIES
#13 KIDNAPPED!
#14 DECEPTIONS
#15 PROMISES
#16 RAGS TO RICHES
#17 LOVE LETTERS
#18 HEAD OVER HEELS
#19 SHOWDOWN
#20 CRASH LANDING!
#21 RUNAWAY
#22 TOO MUCH IN LOVE
#23 SAY GOODBYE
#24 MEMORIES
#25 NOWHERE TO RUN
#26 HOSTAGE!
#27 LOVESTRUCK
#28 ALONE IN THE CROWD
#29 BITTER RIVALS
#30 JEALOUS LIES
#31 TAKING SIDES
#32 THE NEW JESSICA
#33 STARTING OVER
#34 FORBIDDEN LOVE
#35 OUT OF CONTROL
#36 LAST CHANCE
#37 RUMORS
#38 LEAVING HOME
#39 SECRET ADMIRER
#40 ON THE EDGE
#41 OUTCAST
#42 CAUGHT IN THE MIDDLE
#43 HARD CHOICES
#44 PRETENSES
#45 FAMILY SECRETS
#46 DECISIONS
#47 TROUBLEMAKER
#48 SLAM BOOK FEVER
#49 PLAYING FOR KEEPS
#50 OUT OF REACH
#51 AGAINST THE ODDS
#52 WHITE LIES
#53 SECOND CHANCE
#54 TWO-BOY WEEKEND
#55 PERFECT SHOT
#56 LOST AT SEA
#57 TEACHER CRUSH

Super Editions: PERFECT SUMMER
SPECIAL CHRISTMAS
SPRING BREAK
MALIBU SUMMER
WINTER CARNIVAL
SPRING FEVER

Super Thrillers: DOUBLE JEOPARDY
ON THE RUN
NO PLACE TO HIDE
DEADLY SUMMER

SWEET VALLEY HIGH

TEACHER CRUSH

Written by
Kate William

Created by
FRANCINE PASCAL

BANTAM BOOKS
NEW YORK • TORONTO • LONDON • SYDNEY • AUCKLAND

RL 6, IL age 12 and up

TEACHER CRUSH
A Bantam Book / August 1989

Sweet Valley High is a registered trademark of Francine Pascal.

Conceived by Francine Pascal

Produced by Daniel Weiss Associates, Inc.,
27 West 20th Street, New York, NY 10011

Cover art by James Mathewuse

All rights reserved.
Copyright © 1989 by Francine Pascal.
Cover art copyright © 1989 by Daniel Weiss Associates, Inc.
No part of this book may be reproduced or transmitted in any form or by any means, electronic or mechanical, including photocopying, recording, or by any information storage and retrieval system, without permission in writing from the publisher.
For information address: Bantam Books.

ISBN 0-553-28079-1

Published simultaneously in the United States and Canada

Bantam Books are published by Bantam Books, a division of Bantam Doubleday Dell Publishing Group, Inc. Its trademark, consisting of the words "Bantam Books" and the portrayal of a rooster, is Registered in U.S. Patent and Trademark Office and in other countries. Marca Registrada. Bantam Books, 666 Fifth Avenue, New York, New York 10103.

PRINTED IN THE UNITED STATES OF AMERICA

O 0 9 8 7 6 5 4 3 2 1

TEACHER CRUSH

One

"I can't *wait* for minicourses to start!" Jessica Wakefield exclaimed. "Just think, no grades—and interesting courses for once. Plus, math class will be five minutes shorter every day!"

The group of juniors gathered around the lunch table burst out laughing. Jessica was never one to hide an opinion. Everyone was excited about the brand-new series of workshops being offered at Sweet Valley High, but Jessica was one of the most outspoken.

"I'm signing up for dress design," Lila Fowler said, looking over the list of workshops that would be available as part of the Arts and Vocations program.

Jessica took a bite of salad. "Just what you need, more clothes," she grumbled. Lila was the only daughter of one of the wealthiest men in Sweet Valley, and Jessica never forgot for one minute that Lila's closet was almost as big as her own bedroom.

Elizabeth, Jessica's twin sister, was reading her own copy of the Arts and Vocations workshop list. "You're right, Jess," she said. "This is going to be great. We're so lucky to have a chance to take part in this kind of program!" She turned to Enid Rollins, her best friend. "Let's sign up for something together. Which do you think sounds better, painting, pottery, or jewelry design?"

"Painting," Enid said promptly. "But don't you want to wait and see what Jeffrey's signing up for?"

Jeffrey French was Elizabeth's steady boyfriend. "No way," Elizabeth said, shaking her head. "Jeffrey's already told me he wants to take the electronics workshop." She wrinkled her nose. "He's on his own for that one."

"Yeah, but just think," Jessica said with a sigh. "I bet only boys will sign up for that class. I think that's the kind of minicourse to go for. Not something with a zillion girls in it like dress design."

Lila burst out laughing. "Why don't you suggest your own workshop, Jess? Something like 'boys and dating'?"

" 'Advanced boys and dating,' " Amy Sutton murmured, studying the list.

Jessica ignored her friends. "The only one

that sounds any good to me is filmmaking," she said finally. "Only I'd rather star in the film than make it. Running around with a video camera isn't really my idea of fun."

Lila put her list down. "Speaking of film stars," she began, her eyes shining, "did I tell you that my father went out with Anika Hunt again last night? He took her to this really chic little restaurant in Hollywood, and Daddy said it was incredible. She knew every single star who came in, and they all knew her, too."

Jessica's good mood quickly turned sour. For the past week Lila had been bragging about Anika Hunt at every opportunity. Jessica didn't want to hear one more detail about how great Lila's life was and how special she felt now that her father was dating the star of the hottest daytime soap opera, "The Willoughbys."

"I don't believe your father's even met Anika Hunt," Jessica said with a pout. "Can't you bring us something like an autographed picture to prove it?"

Lila was furious. "I don't have to prove anything to you. And I'm not going to ask Anika for her autograph. That's totally babyish."

Jessica rolled her eyes.

"Are you calling me a liar?" Lila demanded. "OK, then. I *will* prove it," she retorted.

"What are you going to do? Bring us her hat?" Jessica asked with a giggle. Amy Sutton laughed, and Jessica felt that she had won the argument. Lila just shrugged.

"Fine. If you don't believe me, don't. Anyway," she added with a smile, "I don't need to sign up for filmmaking. Anika has so many friends in the industry, she can get me a visitor's pass to any Hollywood set I want." She grabbed a pen and began filling in her application form. "So I'll just go right ahead and sign up for dress design."

Jessica frowned at her list. "What happens with these? Are we really starting the workshops on Monday?"

Elizabeth nodded. "The teachers involved in the program are going to assign each student to one of the workshops of their choice over the weekend. Then Monday morning there'll be a list posted of who got what. The plan is to take five minutes off each class hour and lunch, plus add an additional ten minutes, so we'll have a fifty-minute period for the workshop at the end of each day."

Enid, Amy, and Lila all grinned. "Typical Wakefield twins," Amy Sutton said. "How come Elizabeth knows exactly what's going on and Jessica looks like she just dropped in from Mars?"

Jessica wrote "filmmaking" as her first choice. "I'd better get what I want," she muttered. "On second thought, this doesn't sound so great. Whose idea was this workshop thing, anyway?"

"I think it's something the PTA came up

with, along with a group of vocational counselors," Enid told her. "The idea is to run pilot programs in high schools so that we can get intense, two-week training in something we wouldn't ordinarily get to do."

"Electronics, Jess. Put it down," Lila teased.

"I don't think that's such a joke. I *am* putting it down—just not as my first choice," Jessica said huffily. "Why not?" she added when her friends looked shocked. "It would probably be good for me to learn how to make a radio or something like that!"

"I don't know, Jess. It just doesn't seem like your kind of thing," Amy commented.

Jessica wrote "pottery" under second choice. "I want to make one of the gorgeous vases like I saw at the crafts show in the mall last week," she told Amy.

"Dress design is going to be great. Put that down third," Lila urged her. "At the end of the two weeks, we get to model whatever we've made!"

Jessica shrugged. "Who wants to wear what you make? I'm putting electronics third, and dress design fourth." She filled in her form with a dramatic flair, and everyone clapped.

Elizabeth shook her head. "You'd better hope you get your first or second choice, Jess. Two weeks can seem like a long time if you get stuck."

Jessica wrinkled her brow. "Don't play older

sister with me, Liz. I know what I'm doing," she said.

It was a running joke between the twins to refer to each other as the older or younger sister. Elizabeth had been born only four minutes earlier than Jessica, but she often did seem like the older, more responsible twin.

Elizabeth and Jessica were interchangeable as far as appearance went. They were both slender and pretty and had shoulder-length silky blond hair, golden tans, and eyes the color of the blue-green Pacific. They were like mirror images—clones, according to their older brother, Steven. Each showed a tiny dimple when she smiled, and both wore matching gold necklaces, presents from their parents on their sixteenth birthdays. But that ended *identical* as far as either of them was concerned.

Elizabeth was the serious, hardworking twin. She wanted to be a writer one day and spent much of her spare time writing articles for *The Oracle,* Sweet Valley High's school paper. She loved to read and to spend time alone, and although she had many friends, she most enjoyed herself in small groups.

Jessica was the complete opposite. She rarely sat still long enough to read a book, and she would never dream of writing for the school paper. She was much more interested in the social aspects of high school, and for that reason she was co-captain of the cheerleading squad and president of her sorority, Pi Beta Alpha. She loved change and thrived on excitement, and wherever the action was, Jessica was bound to be in the middle of it.

But in spite of their differences, Jessica and Elizabeth were as close as any two people could be, and they would do anything for each other.

Now Jessica caught her twin's eye across the table, and they both smiled.

"My twin, the electronics genius," Elizabeth said.

Jessica didn't feel one bit daunted as she folded up her application for the workshop. She was sure she would get her first choice. And once she met some important people in the film industry, she would be able to prove, once and for all, that Lila had made up the whole story about her father and Anika Hunt!

"Jeffrey," Elizabeth said later that afternoon when they were in the *Oracle* office, "did you really decide on electronics as your first choice for a workshop?" She gave him a teasing smile. "My boyfriend's turning into a high-tech nerd right before my eyes!"

Jeffrey rumpled her hair. "I want to learn more about computers, silly. I promise I won't turn into a nerd." He leaned over and gave her a kiss.

Just then the door to the newspaper office

opened, and Olivia Davidson poked her head inside. "Whoops!" she said.

Elizabeth and Jeffrey pulled apart. They both looked sheepish.

"Don't mind me," Olivia said, smiling. "I just came in to pick up some artwork for next week's paper." Olivia was the arts editor for *The Oracle*. She came into the office and looked through the box that had her name on it. "I hope these workshops inspire some new people to contribute to the paper," she added, riffling through the contributions. "We ought to have more artistic talent around this school than we do."

Elizabeth looked curiously at Olivia. She had always liked her. With her brown halo of frizzy hair, her hazel eyes, her slender frame, and her bohemian clothing, she had a fragile beauty. Olivia was shy and a true free spirit. She didn't seem to care at all what others thought of her. Although she and Elizabeth were good friends, Elizabeth found her slightly mysterious—not like Enid, whom she knew almost as well as she knew herself. "What workshop did you sign up for, Olivia?" she asked.

"Painting." Olivia gave Elizabeth a self-deprecating smile. "I doubt that I'll be much good at it, but I love art, and I really want to learn more about technique." She shrugged. "But I might not get my first choice, anyway."

"Well, I signed up for painting, too. So did

Enid," Elizabeth told her. "Maybe we'll all end up in the same workshop."

Jeffrey picked up the camera from the file cabinet beside him. "I'm going to let you two talk painting. I promised Mr. Collins that I'd get some photographs done." He leaned over again and kissed Elizabeth on the cheek. "See you tonight?" he asked tenderly.

Giving him a little smile, she said softly, "Sure thing."

Olivia silently watched this exchange. For several minutes after Jeffrey left, she continued to sort through her box. Then she turned to look at Elizabeth, her hazel eyes slightly accusing. "Liz," she said, "you are so lucky to have a boyfriend!"

"What do you mean?" Elizabeth asked, surprised.

Olivia shrugged. "You know—someone who loves you the way Jeffrey does." She dropped her eyes, looking shy again, as if she had said something she hadn't intended.

Elizabeth frowned. "Well, it's nice having someone you really care about," she admitted, wondering what was really behind Olivia's outburst.

"It's been such a long time since Roger and I broke up," Olivia continued sadly, still not meeting Elizabeth's eyes. "Sometimes I feel that I'm never going to meet anyone else I care about."

Elizabeth laughed. "That's crazy, Olivia. You're

an incredible girl. You're going to have lots and lots of boyfriends."

"How can you say that?" Olivia demanded. "It's one thing for you—first you went out with Todd, then Jeffrey. You don't know what it's like not having a boyfriend!"

Elizabeth felt a deep blush spread across her face. The fact was, she *had* been involved with Jeffrey for a long time, and before that, Todd Wilkins, her first boyfriend. . . . But Elizabeth still thought of herself as independent. She didn't feel she needed a boyfriend to be happy, the way Olivia seemed to feel.

"Sometimes I get so lonely I can't stand it," Olivia continued. "If I had a boyfriend, everything would be great. I'd have someone to hang around with on weekends and wouldn't feel so lonely all the time."

"Olivia, you can still feel lonely even if you do have a boyfriend," Elizabeth said firmly. "And it's nuts to think that having a boyfriend makes all your troubles vanish!"

Olivia shrugged, as if she didn't believe it. "Well, it would make a *lot* of them vanish," she said quietly. "Everyone I know is part of a couple. This school feels like Noah's ark or something. And I'm the only one who doesn't belong on board!"

"Oh, Olivia," Elizabeth said, jumping up to put an arm around her friend.

But Olivia just looked at her with big sad

eyes. Elizabeth had the sense that nothing she could do or say would make her friend feel any better.

She'd had no idea that Olivia had been feeling so down. Olivia was such a pretty, talented girl. Why should she need to have a boyfriend to feel happy?

Elizabeth wished there was some way she could convey all these thoughts to Olivia. But before she could say a word, Olivia swept up the papers she had been studying and hurried out the door.

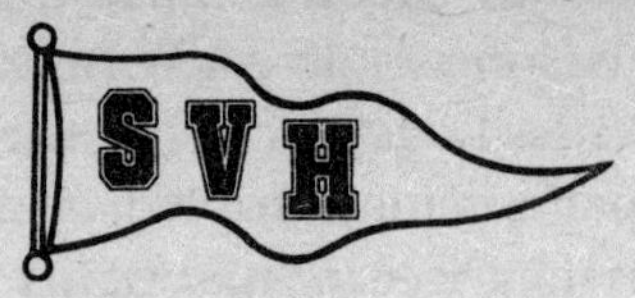

Two

"It's so strange," Elizabeth confided to Enid as the two girls drove to Sweet Valley High on Monday morning. Usually Jessica and Elizabeth went to school together, but Jessica had gotten a ride with Cara Walker, another cheerleader. That had given Elizabeth the opportunity to talk to her best friend about Olivia. "I never had the impression before that Olivia minded not having a boyfriend. Did you?"

Enid shook her head. "No. She seems so self-sufficient. I guess that's partly because she's so into the paper and being arts editor and everything. She seemed that way even when she was going out with Roger. But you should know better than I do, Liz. You and Olivia are really good friends."

Elizabeth was thoughtful. Roger Barrett Patman had been Olivia's boyfriend for quite a while—back in the days when he was Roger Barrett, before it was revealed that he was really the nephew of one of the wealthiest men in the valley. When Roger's mother died of heart disease, the Patmans adopted him. At first the overnight change in his status was hard on Olivia, but eventually the couple worked out their difficulties. It was a surprise to everyone when they finally broke up.

"They always seemed so happy to me," Enid mused.

Elizabeth shrugged. "I don't know. It's so hard to tell what a couple is really like from the outside," she said philosophically. "What I find strange is that all of a sudden Olivia really seems bothered about being on her own. I wonder why."

Enid shook her head. "I don't know. But it doesn't surprise me that much. So many of the girls we know at school have boyfriends. No wonder Olivia feels left out. And I don't blame her for feeling a twinge of jealousy about you and Jeffrey," she added. "You two are such a perfect couple."

Elizabeth blushed as she pulled into the school parking lot. She and Enid got out of the car and were approaching the school building when she saw Olivia walking toward them.

"Hi," Olivia said, falling into step beside them. "Are you guys psyched for the first day of workshops?"

Enid nodded. "I really hope I get into the painting class."

"That's the one I'm hoping for, too," Olivia said. She glanced across the parking lot, her gaze falling on DeeDee Gordon and Bill Chase walking into the school building arm in arm. They were just behind Maria Santelli and Winston Egbert, who were holding hands. Olivia frowned. "I bet everyone's signing up for the workshops in couples," she muttered.

Enid gave Elizabeth a look that said clearly, "I see what you mean." "That isn't true, Olivia," Enid said quickly. "Elizabeth and Jeffrey didn't sign up for the same workshop!"

"That's right." Elizabeth wrinkled her nose. "I couldn't get excited about taking radios or computers apart for two whole weeks."

Olivia shrugged but didn't answer. And before Elizabeth could say another word about Jeffrey, he had bounded up and given her a big hug. Elizabeth grinned at him, so glad to see him that she barely caught the frown on Olivia's face as she turned away.

"What's wrong with Olivia?" Jeffrey asked after she had trudged up the walk into the building by herself.

"She has a bad case of wish-I-had-a-boyfriend blues," Enid said, sighing. "She really seems pretty lonesome. I wonder—"

But Jeffrey cut her off. "I can't imagine Olivia

being lonesome. She has so many friends and so many interests."

Enid shrugged. "I don't know. I can sympathize with her. I know what it was like before I was going out with Hugh." Enid's boyfriend, Hugh Grayson, attended high school in another town not far from Sweet Valley. "There were times when it seemed to me like the whole world was filled with couples. That can make you feel pretty lonesome."

Elizabeth took Jeffrey's hand and squeezed it. She knew how lucky she was to be in love, especially with someone as wonderful and considerate as Jeffrey. But while she agreed with Enid, she secretly felt that Olivia's behavior wasn't characteristic of her. She wondered why it suddenly seemed so important to Olivia to have a special guy around.

After all, she had known Olivia for a long time. She had never seen signs of this kind of neediness before.

"Come on, Liz. Let's go in and see what workshops we got assigned to," Jeffrey said, tugging at her hand.

Elizabeth quickened her pace. She couldn't believe it. She had gotten so wrapped up in thinking about Olivia, she had almost forgotten that the list would be posted!

Jessica pushed through the crowd in front of

the bulletin board. Everyone was peering at the workshop lists, writing down the room where he or she would be meeting that day. From the excited cries around her, it sounded as if most people had gotten what they wanted.

"Dress designing—Lila Fowler," Lila crowed.

Winston Egbert, widely acknowledged as the clown of the junior class, decided to play emcee and started reading people's names off the list. "Electronics is going to be the best one by far," he insisted. "How can it go wrong? It's got me at the head of the list!"

"Move it, Egbert. You're blocking the view," Ken Matthews joked, trying to get closer to the board.

"Hey, Jeffrey, we're in electronics together!" Winston cried, seeing Jeffrey French's name on the list.

Enid turned back to Elizabeth with a big smile. "We got in," she told her friend. "And so did you, Olivia! We all got into painting!"

Jessica squinted up at the list, trying to find her name under filmmaking. Why wasn't it there? Had someone made a mistake?

"Darn. I got pottery instead of painting," Cara Walker said, looking dismayed.

"I didn't get my first choice, either," Maria Santelli said. "I got nutrition and fitness instead of modern dance."

Jessica frowned. "Well, looks like I didn't get

filmmaking," she muttered, inching over to study the list under pottery.

Just then Winston let out an incredible whoop. "Jessica Wakefield, electronics!"

Jessica stared at him. "That isn't funny, Winston," she said coldly, pressing in for a closer look.

"Who's trying to be funny?" Winston pretended to be hurt.

Jessica felt the color drain from her face. "I can't believe it," she cried. "Everyone else got at least their second choice! And I got stuck with electronics!" She wouldn't have minded if there had been a couple of cute guys in the class, but as she looked down the list, she didn't recognize a single name except Jeffrey's and Winston's. And she knew the name of every cute guy in the school.

"*Stuck*?" Winston repeated comically. "You got into the best workshop of the bunch, Jess."

Lila, Cara, and Amy were all doubling up with laughter. "I can't wait to see what you're going to make, Jess," Lila scoffed.

"Maybe you can *make* a video camera instead of using one," Amy teased.

Elizabeth gave her twin a consoling pat on the arm. "Don't worry, Jess. I'm sure it'll be really fun, and you'll learn a lot."

Jessica's eyes flashed furiously. "I can't believe it. I'm going to complain," she added. "It isn't fair, getting stuck with my third choice."

"Look on the bright side," Jeffrey said, giving her a big smile. "You get to be in the class with Winston and me."

"Terrific," she said moodily. "Everyone else is going to be having a great time, and I'm going to be taking apart a television or something terrible like that."

The bell rang then, and everyone moved down the hall together toward the auditorium, where a special assembly was being held to introduce the workshop teachers. Jessica lagged behind, staring disconsolately at her name on the list.

She couldn't believe it. She just couldn't believe what rotten luck this was. For two terrible weeks she was going to be stuck in electronics unless she could think of some way to wriggle out of it!

Mr. Collins and Mr. Jaworski, who taught respectively English and history, were the two main speakers at that morning's assembly. When Mr. Collins got up to speak, everyone clapped and cheered. The blond, handsome Robert Redford look-alike was one of the most popular teachers at school.

"Good morning," he said into the microphone, looking around the crowded auditorium. "We called this assembly because we wanted to introduce the special program we're running for the junior and senior classes here at Sweet Valley High, in conjunction with the PTA and with local artists and vocational instructors." Everyone clapped again when he added, "I think you'll all agree with me that we are very lucky to have been chosen to take part in this program, designed to help integrate extracurricular learning into our schools."

"Yeah," Jessica muttered to Amy and Lila. "Extracurricular electronics. Really great."

Lila was busily thumbing through the latest issue of *Ingenue* magazine. "Look at this," she said, passing the magazine to Jessica. She had folded down a page where a beautiful model was wearing a strapless sun dress, a matching jacket draped over one arm. "This is exactly what I want to make in the dress design workshop. Just the dress, that is. Not the jacket. It would take too long."

Jessica casually glanced at the photograph. "It looks almost exactly like that dress I bought at the mall two weeks ago. Doesn't it?" she asked Amy.

Lila didn't seem disturbed by this piece of information. "Well, this is what I'm going to make," she declared.

Amy giggled. "Maybe Jessica can make one of those electronic devices that beep if you try to leave a store without having the tag removed from your purchase."

Jessica slumped down in her seat. She didn't appreciate her friends making fun of her predicament. From the way it sounded, everyone except her was going to be having a wonderful time in the workshops!

Mr. Collins cleared his throat. "Now, I want to remind you all how the program will be structured. Workshops begin today, last period. Don't forget: each class and lunch period will end five minutes early for the next two weeks in order to make time for workshops. And each of you will be working on a constructive workshop project, whether it's practical, creative, or both. You'll probably have to do work outside of class too, if your project is complicated. In order to give you all a chance to see each others' work, we've decided to hold a school-wide fair the last day of the workshops. That will be a week from Friday. Each of you will be expected to present the final product from your workshop at that point."

Everyone cheered at this. "I can't wait to model my dress," Lila said, eyeing the model in the magazine. But Mr. Collins was putting up his hand to calm down the crowd.

"Now, if you'll all be patient, we'd like to introduce the teachers of each workshop. Most of them are from the area, though a few have come from San Diego or Los Angeles. You'll be seeing them all in the halls and at lunchtime, so we want you to recognize them." Mr. Collins nodded to the group sitting near him on the stage, and one by one the workshop teachers stood up to be introduced.

"Elinore Whitcomb will be teaching dress design," Mr. Collins said, introducing a svelte, stylish woman with a friendly smile. Lila clapped so hard, the magazine fell off her lap.

"She looks a little like Anika Hunt," Lila whispered to Amy. Jessica ignored them. She was watching sadly as Mr. Collins introduced Bill Drexel, the electronics teacher. He looked every bit as bad as she had feared he would: skinny, with little round wire-rimmed glasses that sat crookedly on his nose. He wore a drab, nondescript suit.

"He sure looks like a barrel of laughs," Jessica grumbled.

"Whoa," Lila gasped, grabbing Jessica's arm. "Who is *that*?"

Jessica followed her gaze. Roger Collins was smiling at a young man who'd stood up to be introduced to the roomful of students. "Now, for all you artists, I'd like to introduce Stuart Bachman, a local painter. He'll be teaching the painting workshop."

Jessica's blue-green eyes widened. It was hard to believe Stuart Bachman could live on the same planet as Bill Drexel. He was incredibly good-looking, with longish curly, dark hair and stylish glasses. He looked mysterious, artistic, *fascinating*.

"It isn't fair," Jessica grumbled again. "I can't believe my very own twin sister gets to take a workshop from that gorgeous man while I'm stuck with a teacher who looks like a worm."

Lila giggled. "Hey," she said, inspired, "maybe you can dress like Liz for the next two weeks and try to sneak into the painting workshop."

Jessica shook her head despairingly. "Liz isn't going to switch with me. Are you kidding? She'd be out of her mind to give up a class with anyone who looks like that."

Lila nodded sagely. "Cheer up, Jess," she said with a grin. "Maybe you can invent something like a mental telepathy helmet. Or a dream machine." She giggled. "Then you can *dream* your way into Stuart Bachman's workshop!"

"Very funny," Jessica said, rolling her eyes.

Lila Fowler was really beginning to get on her nerves: first gloating nonstop about Anika Hunt, and now teasing her endlessly about the electronics workshop. Jessica decided it was time to think of some way to put her friend in her place.

But she didn't have long to dwell on the possibilities. Mr. Collins wrapped up his talk, and everyone stood up to go to class. Jessica was heading for the aisle when the girl in front of her stopped suddenly and Jessica bumped into her.

"Sorry," she said, taking a step back.

Then she saw it was Olivia Davidson. Oddly enough, Olivia didn't even seem to have heard Jessica or have felt it when Jessica bumped into her. She was staring straight in front of her, a vacant, dreamy expression on her face; staring straight at Stuart Bachman with a look of complete and utter adoration in her eyes.

Three

"Elizabeth," Olivia whispered nervously, "do you think my hair looks weird like this?" She tugged at her brown, frizzy hair, a look of consternation on her pretty face.

Elizabeth, Enid, and Olivia were in the art room where the painting workshop was taking place. It was two-fifteen on Monday afternoon, and any minute the very first workshop was going to get started. Elizabeth was putting on one of the smocks that Mr. Bachman had left in a pile in the front of the room, and Enid, who already had her smock on, was trying to set up an easel.

"You look fine, Olivia," Elizabeth said.

But Olivia didn't seem to hear her. "Can you guys believe how gorgeous Mr. Bachman is? When I saw him—"

She broke off when the door opened and Mr. Bachman came in. He strolled up to the front of the room, looked around, then smiled. "So, this is it," he said at last. "You're my painting group." He held a clipboard with a list of names on it, and after a minute of looking around, he sat down on the edge of the table in the front of the room and cleared his throat. "Let me just say a couple of things first to introduce myself and the class. My name is Stuart Bachman, but I go by Stuart, *not* Mr. Bachman. I know it's hard to get used to calling a teacher by his first name, but it's my first—and only—rule."

A couple of people laughed, and immediately the atmosphere in the room seemed more relaxed. Stuart smiled. "I'm a painter, as Mr. Collins told you this morning. I've been an artist since I was about five years old." He ran his hand through his long, curly hair and grinned. "But I haven't always been able to make a living at it. So since I graduated from college, I've been working as a graphic designer for a fashion company. I design logos, do some graphics for ads, that kind of thing. But that isn't my passion. My passion—" He broke off and gazed at the group. You could have heard a pin drop in the room. "My passion is painting. That's why I'm here."

Elizabeth nudged Enid, looking past her best friend to the place where Olivia was standing, lips slightly parted, staring at Stuart Bachman. She appeared completely engrossed.

"We're not going to have any rules or regulations in this class—that isn't the point. All I ask is that you each do a painting for me. I'm going to start out by explaining a number of techniques to you, helping you individually with your projects, and supervising your work." Stuart's eyes were very intense. "But the real work has to come from you. Now, I know I don't need to tell any of you that a painting, a real painting, can take an artist anywhere from one day to a lifetime to complete. I don't expect miracles from you. I just want you to use your imaginations. Don't be inhibited. Today, for instance, we're going to do an exercise in color. Does anyone know what that means?"

He was looking straight at Enid. "Does that mean you want us to practice putting different colors next to each other?" she asked.

Stuart smiled. "Yes, that would be one idea. What's your name?" he added, checking his list.

"Enid Rollins," Enid said promptly.

"OK, Enid. That's great. Does anyone else have an idea of what a good color exercise might be?"

Caroline Pearce raised her hand. "What about trying to paint different shades of the same color?" she suggested.

"Very good," Mr. Bachman said, looking pleased. He went around the room and then asked each of the ten students in the workshop to give their suggestions for what a color exercise might be. When he came to Olivia, she turned scarlet and stared at the floor.

"I don't know if this is right or not," she murmured. "But maybe you could ask people to paint a color without really using that color at all."

Caroline Pearce tittered and poked Maria Santelli in the side. But Mr. Bachman was looking very seriously at Olivia.

"What do you mean?" he asked intently. "I'm sorry, your name is—"

"Olivia Davidson," she whispered, her face still bright red. "What I meant was . . . well, if you could try to figure out a way to paint a color, say, green, without really using green to do it . . ."

Mr. Bachman cleared his throat and looked at her with a surprised smile. "Actually, Olivia, you've just guessed my very first assignment," he said. "Today I would like you all to paint the color green without using any green paint." His smile seemed to single Olivia out, as if her idea were especially interesting. Everyone else looked puzzled.

"Well, I don't really see how we're going to do it," Enid said to Elizabeth. "But I guess it's worth a try."

Elizabeth didn't answer. She was looking at Olivia, who was staring unabashedly at Mr. Bachman.

It was as if she were transfixed, standing there and watching him with shining eyes. Elizabeth had the feeling that nothing in the world could shake Olivia from where she was standing.

Jessica couldn't believe her eyes when she opened the door to the electronics workshop. There were eight boys sitting patiently in front of Bill Drexel, and they all looked like total nerds to her. She sat down between Winston and Jeffrey. This was going to be even worse than she had feared.

Bill Drexel was telling them all that he worked for an electronics firm. "But I don't expect any of you to design a computer," he said. Everyone but Jessica laughed.

"Here's what I do expect," he went on. "You each have two weeks to design and create a project. I'll be here to help you all I can. Do any of you have an idea right now about what you'd like to work on?"

To Jessica's horror, most of them did. Jeffrey said he wanted to write his own computer game. The nerdiest boy in the entire class, Randy Mason, said he wanted to make a robotic calculator.

"A what?" Jessica asked.

"I want to make sure all my equations are done with perfect accuracy," Randy said.

Winston, never one to lose an opportunity for a joke, listed several things he wanted to make: a musical toaster, an electric page-turner, a voice-activated coffee maker. Bill Drexel looked at him with alarm. Finally he turned to Jessica.

"I'm glad to see we have a young lady in this class," he said warmly. "Too few women enroll in courses like this. What do you intend to make?"

Jessica cleared her throat. She couldn't think of a single thing she wanted to design, let alone figure out how to make it. "I—uh, I'm not sure," she said weakly.

Winston poked her in the arm. "How about an electronic perfume-applier?" he said.

Jessica gave him a withering stare. At that point the last thing in the world she wanted to be subjected to was Winston Egbert's sick sense of humor.

"Well, you'll all have a day or two to think it over," Mr. Drexel said. "But I want you to get started right away. We only have two weeks, and as I'm sure you all know, that's not very long when you have a technological project to work on!"

Jessica slumped down low in her seat. Somehow she couldn't see it that way. The more she thought about it, the longer two weeks seemed.

Olivia stepped back from her easel and looked critically at her painting. She had spent almost the entire first class doing the color exercise, but she couldn't tell whether or not she had succeeded. She had tried to paint a garden, using blues and browns to convey the feeling of green.

Mr. Bachman was strolling around the room, stopping to comment on each student's work. The closer he came to Olivia, the more nervous she got.

She couldn't believe the way he made her feel. Her hands felt sweaty, her throat was dry. She felt about twelve years old, not sixteen.

Mr. Bachman was looking at Elizabeth's canvas now, right next to Olivia. "That's nice, Elizabeth," he said, squinting seriously at the canvas.

Olivia swallowed hard. She was next.

For several minutes Mr. Bachman stood behind her, looking over her work. He didn't say anything, he just studied the swirls of blue, the solid brown lines. Then, clearing his throat, he said, "This is wonderful, Olivia. Have you taken painting classes before?"

His voice was low, and Olivia didn't think anyone else had heard him. Her cheeks burned as she said, "Well, I, uh, took some watercolor lessons last year at the community center, but I've never worked with acrylics before. I like art a lot, though—you know, going to museums and stuff. But I'm really just a beginner."

"Well, you'd never know it from looking at this," Mr. Bachman said seriously. He leaned closer to examine the arc of different-colored hues Olivia had painted, and she could smell his after-shave. Her blush deepened.

"I hope we're not going to be holding you back in here," Mr. Bachman murmured. He didn't seem to notice that she was bright red and standing rigid with joy and alarm at having him so close. "I'll tell you what," he added, looking directly at her. His eyes, behind his glasses, were green. Garden green, Olivia thought. "You decide what kind of painting you want to do for the next two weeks, and no matter how difficult or ambitious, I'll help you with it. OK?"

It seemed to take every bit of effort Olivia could muster just to murmur back, "OK."

When Mr. Bachman had moved out of earshot, Elizabeth came over to inspect Olivia's work. "That's terrific, Liv!" she cried enthusiastically.

Sighing, Olivia set her paintbrush down. A storm of emotions was running through her. On the one hand she wanted to come up with a painting that would impress Stuart, really impress him. But on the other hand she was afraid nothing she could ever do could possibly be good enough.

She wanted to know everything about Stuart Bachman. Where he lived. What kind of paintings he liked. What his own paintings were like. She couldn't bear to take her eyes off him for a single second.

"Olivia?" Elizabeth was saying, a puzzled

frown on her face. "Didn't you hear me? I asked if you had any plans yet for your final painting."

Olivia shook her head. "No, I don't."

The other students started cleaning up, gathering their things. Olivia went through the motions as quickly as she could. Just knowing Stuart was in the room made her feel clumsy.

A few minutes later, Enid and Elizabeth were heading down the hall toward their lockers when they noticed Olivia walking ahead of them.

"So, what did you guys think?" Enid asked, catching up with Olivia.

"I think Mr. Bach— I mean Stuart, is going to be a wonderful teacher," Elizabeth said. "He so obviously cares about painting—and about us."

For a brief instant Olivia felt stricken. Did Stuart care about all of them equally? Had she imagined that he had singled her out? Or was there—was she completely wrong in hoping—a real connection between them?

"Olivia, you're awfully quiet today," Elizabeth said. "What did you think of the class?"

Olivia bit her lip. The next minute she blurted out, "I think Stuart Bachman is the most wonderful man I've ever met!"

Elizabeth and Enid stared at each other, obviously taken aback by the force of her outburst. Olivia blushed and added, "I mean, he's so dedicated. And Liz is right. He seems like an excellent teacher."

But she could tell she had already given herself away. It wasn't surprising, either. Feeling the way she did, Olivia expected that in no time at all that the whole world would know that she was in love with Stuart Bachman. Madly in love. And she could barely endure the agony of waiting a full day until she got to see him again.

Four

Lila was raving again on Wednesday about Anika Hunt. "Can you imagine?" she gushed at lunchtime. "If she and Daddy get married, I'll be the stepdaughter of a movie star!"

Jessica rolled her eyes. "Right," she muttered. "I bet that happens the same day I turn out to have a hidden talent for electronics!"

Lila ignored this jibe. "Speaking of minicourses, dress design is wonderful," she continued. "Elinore is the *best*. And she loved my idea for a dress."

"You didn't happen to tell her that I own one almost exactly like it, did you?" Jessica asked.

Lila shook her head. "I don't think originality is the most important point, Jess. We're learning all about material and sewing. Stuff like that."

Jessica shrugged. She was about to comment when she saw something that made her eyebrows shoot up. "Hey, speaking of dress designing," she exclaimed, "get a load of what Olivia Davidson is wearing!"

Lila turned her head to follow Jessica's gaze. Olivia looked like a completely different person. Usually she wore a variation on the same theme: a peasant-style wrap skirt, a pastel-colored T-shirt, sandals, lots of beads, and big hoop earrings. But she was obviously trying to change her image. Today she was wearing a body-hugging black dress, leather boots and a leather jacket, and her hair was styled with gel. She looked very fashionable—sleek and interesting. Everything about her appearance said that she wanted to be noticed.

Elizabeth and Enid were having lunch with Jeffrey on the other side of the lunchroom when they saw Olivia walk past.

Enid clasped one hand over her mouth. "I don't believe it! Look at Olivia! She looks like she just stepped right out of a fashion magazine."

Elizabeth's eyes widened incredulously. "Olivia!" she called, waving her over.

Olivia hurried across the room and plopped down at their table. Several art magazines spilled out of her notebook as she set it down. "Hi," she said breathlessly, one hand flying up to adjust a large, triangular-shaped earring. "What do you guys think? Do I look more—you know, sophisticated?"

Elizabeth gave her a big smile. "You look

absolutely great." She couldn't get over the change in Olivia. She looked so radiantly happy!

"I think you look great, too," Jeffrey said. "But, uh, where did you get those earrings, Liv? They look kind of like they hurt."

"Oh, just some little boutique," Olivia said casually. She tugged on her ear. "Those hoops I was wearing before were so, you know, juvenile."

Elizabeth leaned closer to inspect her friend's new earrings. "Those are really wonderful!" she exclaimed.

Olivia nodded rapturously. "I've been getting all sorts of cool ideas from these magazines. Have you guys ever read *Art World* before? Or *Art Adventure*? Or this one—this is my favorite." She showed them a copy of a magazine simply called *A*. "It's completely cool." She turned to the center of the magazine. "And look at this! An interview with you-know-who."

Elizabeth and Enid crowded closer to see. Sure enough, there was an interview with Stuart Bachman.

"Wow, he looks great there," Enid said.

Olivia stared dreamily at the magazine. "Yeah, doesn't he?" she said.

Elizabeth bent over the magazine to see the photograph of Stuart. Before she could get a good look, Olivia scooped up her magazines and jumped up, her eyes shining. "I don't have time to eat," she declared. "Stuart said he'd be available to talk about the class during lunch, and I have lots of questions. Did you guys know Stuart and I have the same favorite artist? David Hockney. It says so in this interview." Olivia hugged the magazine. "I can't wait to tell him what a coincidence it is!"

With that Olivia hurried off, leaving Elizabeth, Enid, and Jeffrey staring after her in disbelief.

It turned out that Stuart Bachman wasn't in the library as Olivia had expected. He was using the art room as a studio during the day, and it took Olivia almost twenty minutes to find him. When she knocked on the door, he didn't seem to hear her, so she timidly opened it and tiptoed inside.

Stuart had his back to her. He appeared to be hard at work on a large abstract oil painting, and for several minutes Olivia just watched him while he frowned at the painting. Then, feeling like a trespasser, she cleared her throat. Stuart jumped.

"Oh, hi, Olivia. Come on in," he said. If he noticed her different look, he didn't comment on it.

Olivia walked slowly toward the canvas, staring at it. She didn't know how to describe the way it made her feel, but the startling colors and shapes were full of life and vibrancy. "What a wonderful painting," she said softly.

Stuart looked at the work. "Thank you. I like it, too." He smiled. "I feel OK about admitting that, since for every painting I do that I like, there must be about a dozen that I have to junk."

Olivia was horrified. "You mean you throw something out that you've put that much trouble into?"

Stuart shrugged. "That's the way art is. It's an unforgiving business," he told her. His eyes were so warm and compassionate that Olivia didn't feel the slightest bit strange asking him how long he had wanted to be an artist.

"Ever since I can remember," he told her. "It didn't exactly run in my family, either. My dad is a history professor, and my mother's a bookkeeper. I don't think they quite knew what to do with me when I started messing around with paints."

Olivia laughed, her shyness evaporating. He was so easy to talk to! "Is it hard sometimes," she asked next, feeling braver, "finding something to inspire you?" The minute the question was out, she blushed. It sounded much more daring and personal than she had intended.

Stuart didn't seem to take it that way, though. He was quiet for a minute. Then he shook his head. "I don't know where the inspiration comes from. But thank God it seems to keep coming. You know, Olivia, I could ask you the same question," he said quietly. "From the way you did that exercise in class yesterday, I know how much talent you must have. Have you been thinking seriously about art for some time now?"

Olivia blushed and shook her head. "I'm the arts editor of the school paper," she said, wishing she had something more impressive to tell him. "But I'm not an artist. I've always loved going to museums, though. I'm crazy about David Hockney, and whenever I look at his work it makes me want to be able to paint. I'd like to paint," she murmured. "I mean, I'd like to learn how."

"Well, you're off to a good start," Stuart said. "I meant what I said yesterday in class, Olivia. I want you to feel free to come by any time to talk about your artwork. I want to give you all the extra help I can. I have a feeling you're going to do something great in this class."

Olivia just stared at him. She couldn't believe her ears. Did that mean he thought she was special, that he liked her as much as she liked him? She could hardly believe how lucky she was. She felt—literally—as if her feet weren't touching the ground.

"Well, uh, I—I guess I'll see you this afternoon, in the workshop," Olivia stammered.

Stuart smiled. And then, before she said another word, he winked at her.

She couldn't believe it. Her stomach did flip-flops, and she had to take a deep breath to steady herself.

Now she knew she wasn't just imagining it. Stuart Bachman really liked her. It was one thing to say she would do great things, but that wink said so much more. She was certain now he thought she was special in another way, not just as a student.

Olivia practically floated out of the studio. All she could think about was that wink and what she hoped—no, *knew*—that it meant.

Elizabeth, Enid, and Jessica were standing around in the hall together during the break between the last class of the day and workshops. Jessica had an expression of such misery on her face that Elizabeth's heart went out to her. "It can't be that bad," she said.

"*Bad*," Jessica declared, "is not the word. Picture sitting next to nerdy Randy Mason. He'll probably try to turn me into a robot before the workshop is over. Plus, I don't have the faintest idea what I'm going to make. So far the only thing I can come up with is a heated coat hanger. And that doesn't seem very useful."

Elizabeth and Enid grinned at each other.

"Well, I'm off to the torture chamber," Jessica grumbled, shifting her books from one arm to the other and plodding sorrowfully in the direction of her electronics workshop.

The minute Jessica was out of earshot, Enid put her hand on Elizabeth's arm and gave her a meaningful look. "Now, remember what I said, Liz. Watch Olivia in class today and tell me what you think."

"All right," Elizabeth said. "But I still don't think she has a real crush on him, Enid. I just think she's excited about painting. She's clearly talented, and I think Stuart's encouraging her to try her hardest."

"I don't know, Liz. I know you always refuse to believe anything less than the very best about people. But remember, Olivia was going on and on about wanting a boyfriend before the workshop even started."

"I still don't see the connection," Elizabeth said. "Olivia's just really excited about art right now, that's all."

Enid frowned. "All I know is, that girl's been acting really strange. Every time I've seen her today the first words out of her mouth have been 'Stuart says' or 'Stuart thinks.' It's a little much."

Elizabeth was just about to defend Olivia when the girl came hurrying up, still struggling with one of her funky earrings. "Come on, you guys," she commanded. "You don't want to be late for painting!"

Elizabeth and Enid fell into step beside Olivia, who chattered on and on. "I can't wait for class. I've been thinking all day long about what kind of painting I want to do, and I can't wait to ask Stuart— Don't you guys just think he's the most adorable guy in the world?"

Enid nudged Elizabeth. "He's a nice-looking man," she said nonchalantly. "But he's a little on the old side. Too old for us, I mean."

"*Old*?" Olivia repeated curiously, as if that hadn't occurred to her before. For a minute she looked crushed, but then her face brightened. "I don't think he's that old. He just graduated from college two years ago, so he's probably only about twenty-three."

"Old," Enid said sagely.

Olivia looked wounded. "What difference does age make when it comes to something as important as art?"

Elizabeth and Enid exchanged glances, but by then they had reached the art room, and their conversation broke off. Stuart gave them a welcoming smile as they entered.

"I'm glad you three are here," he said, looking only at Olivia. "Olivia, I was just telling the rest of the group about your interest in David Hockney. I think I'm going to give you all an extra assignment in this workshop and ask each one of you to go to the Sweet Valley Museum, choose one painting you really like, and write a short essay about what you think the artist was trying to do." He was still looking at Olivia. "Olivia, can you tell the rest of the class a little bit about Hockney and how you came to be interested in him?"

Elizabeth listened quietly to this exchange. She wondered if there was any real basis for

Enid's concern about Olivia. Was it possible that Stuart Bachman was encouraging Olivia without realizing it? Maybe singling her out right now wasn't the best thing he could do.

Not that you'd ever know that from looking at Olivia. She was positively radiant, her eyes glowing as she told the class that she had always been drawn to Hockney because of the way he used colors and shapes.

Elizabeth couldn't see anything wrong with Olivia's excitement, though. Despite Enid's worry, she thought Olivia's enthusiasm was the most natural thing in the world. Olivia had talent and loved art. Why shouldn't she be delighted to be singled out by a talented teacher like Stuart Bachman?

For the rest of the class, Elizabeth watched her friend closely. She still didn't see any reason to be alarmed by Olivia's behavior. It was true that Olivia asked a question any time she had the opportunity. She also volunteered to take down the easels and help Stuart clean up afterward. And she must have asked him his opinion of her sketch for a painting about a dozen times. But why shouldn't she? Elizabeth's feeling was that Olivia wanted to learn everything she could about art and get all she could out of this workshop.

"Look at the way she keeps staring at him," Enid hissed.

Elizabeth gave her friend a reproving look.

"Enid, stop it. She's just being a good student, that's all."

But Enid couldn't shake the notion that Olivia was interested in more than art. For the rest of the class, Enid nudged Elizabeth whenever she saw something that worried her. When the workshop ended and Olivia asked again if she could help him clean up, Mr. Bachman gave her a big smile. "You know, in Europe certain artists are lucky enough to have apprentices. I think you'd make a good apprentice, Olivia."

Olivia looked as if she had just been given the Nobel Prize. Enid poked Elizabeth in the ribs, and Elizabeth giggled.

"OK, Enid. Maybe she's going overboard a tiny little bit. But only because she's trying to be serious about painting."

Elizabeth simply didn't believe that Olivia was doing anything inappropriate. In fact, she was sure Enid was wrong.

Five

Jessica took a deep breath, stopping for a minute in front of the door to the room where the electronics workshop was being held. "Here goes nothing," she muttered, pushing the door open.

It was even worse than she had remembered. There was Mr. Drexel, pacing back and forth in front of the room, looking nerdier than ever as he watched the boys in front of him hard at work on their projects.

Jessica wrinkled her nose. Randy Mason had millions of pieces of copper, little bits of metal, and all sorts of gadgets and tools spread out in front of him. Winston was squinting into a toaster, which he was holding upside down over his head. Jeffrey was hard at work on a computer in the corner of the room.

Mr. Drexel looked at his watch and frowned. "Jessica," he said, "you know our workshop begins promptly at two-fifteen."

Jessica slid into her seat. She knew she was late. But somehow she hadn't been able to drag herself away from study hall. The fact was, she didn't want to come to the workshop at all. "Sorry," she whispered.

"That's all right," Mr. Drexel said, smiling at her. "Before you came in, we were going around the room telling each other about our projects. Have you had any ideas, Jessica?"

Winston grinned, and Jessica bit her lip. "Uh, well, I've been thinking about it really hard," she said lamely.

Winston looked at her with real sympathy. "Poor Jessica. Do you need any help coming up with an idea?"

Jessica didn't like thinking Winston could help her. "No, thanks," she said uncharitably. "At least when I do come up with an idea, it won't be something ridiculous like a singing toaster!"

"It isn't going to be musical, " Winston corrected her. "I decided to make it voice activated instead."

Jessica groaned. Mr. Drexel, ignoring this exchange, gave Jessica a handout and a list of local companies to call for advice on certain projects. She was inspecting it forlornly when he added, "We also teamed up with lab partners before you came in. Jessica, your partner is Randy Mason. Could you move over and share his lab space with him? From now on, you two will be giving each other advice on your projects."

Jessica's eyes widened. She wouldn't have believed a minute ago that things could get worse—and now she was stuck with Randy Mason for a lab partner!

Just looking at him made her want to cry. He was shorter than she was and wore the kind of corduroy jeans nobody wore anymore. Plus, he kept a calculator in his back pocket. Jessica swallowed hard. The workshop was getting harder and harder to bear.

"Why do we need lab partners?" she asked, trying to sound nonchalant.

"I think you'll find it very helpful to have someone to compare notes with," Mr. Drexel said firmly.

Randy smiled at Jessica, and Jessica tried her hardest to smile back. "Well," she said, pulling up a chair and inspecting the mountain of wires and cogs Randy had heaped before him, "I guess I'm your lab partner."

Randy smiled radiantly, exposing two rows of metal braces. Jessica sighed heavily. She didn't know how a boy as small as Randy could manage to lug around all that metal. She looked wistfully at Jeffrey and Winston, wishing she could have been teamed up with one of them. Still, Randy seemed like a nice guy. Maybe it wouldn't be that awful.

Winston obviously found her predicament hilarious. "Jessica Wakefield and Randy Mason—there's a team," he chortled. "Move over,

Rodgers and Hammerstein! Take a bow, Livingstone and Stanley! We've got a partnership here that will revolutionize the world of high technology!"

Jessica glared at him. She was in no mood for his antics right now. All she could do was sit and watch broodingly while Randy deftly moved pieces of wire around.

He seemed to know exactly what he was doing—she had to give him credit for that. As a matter of fact, as she sat and watched him work intently on his project it suddenly struck Jessica that it might not be such a bad idea getting teamed up with Randy Mason.

One thing was clear: There was no way that Jessica was going to be able to make any sort of passable project in this workshop without someone's help.

And it looked like Randy Mason was just going to have to be that someone!

"Stuart," Olivia said eagerly, hurrying to catch up with the artist on Thursday afternoon. "Can I help you set up things for class this afternoon? I have study hall right before, so I wouldn't be missing a class or anything."

Mr. Bachman turned to her and smiled warmly. "That's awfully nice of you, Olivia. You don't need to help me. I'm sure there are lots of things you'd rather be doing during your break."

Olivia blushed. "No, I'd really like to help," she protested.

Mr. Bachman thought it over. "All right. Why don't you meet me at one forty-five, and we can get the easels out of the art storage closets and set them up."

Olivia couldn't believe her luck. An entire half hour alone with Stuart Bachman!

She felt as though her life had completely changed over the course of the past few days. A week ago she didn't even know Stuart Bachman existed, and now he was literally all she thought about. She had gotten his address by checking an alumni catalog at the Riverside Art Academy, where he had been a student. It didn't contain his phone number, but just knowing the name of the street where he lived made her incredibly happy. And she had already cut out his picture from the art magazine and stuck it up on her mirror at home. That photograph was literally the first thing she saw when she woke up in the morning and the last thing before she went to bed.

So far Olivia hadn't told anyone how she felt about Stuart. She knew it wasn't a good idea. After all, he was her instructor, and he was older—though not all that much older, she assured herself. After all, her birthday was coming up—it was a week from tomorrow. She didn't know Stuart's exact age, maybe twenty-two or twenty-three. Not that much older when you came right down to it. Her father was six years older than her mother. In movies guys were almost always older. It was romantic, she decided.

Olivia was deep in thought about Stuart when Elizabeth came up to her, a concerned expression on her face. "Olivia," she said, "have you seen the proofs for the arts pages of *The Oracle*? Mr. Collins said you hadn't turned them in yet. And we have to get the material to the printer no later than tomorrow morning!"

Olivia stared at her. She had completely forgotten about her work for *The Oracle*. For the past few days she had been so completely consumed by thoughts of Stuart and the workshop that she hadn't had time to look over the proofs. As a matter of fact, she had left them at home. "Liz, I can't believe it. I totally forgot!"

Elizabeth looked worried. "Do you have them with you? Maybe we can check them during study hall."

"Look, Liz, I'll go over them tonight, the minute I get home, and drop them off at the printer myself before school tomorrow," Olivia promised. "I don't know what got into me this week, but it'll never happen again, I swear!"

Elizabeth glanced at her. "Well, you should talk to Penny and Mr. Collins about it." Penny Ayala was the editor-in-chief of *The Oracle*. "I don't know what they'll want you to do."

Olivia bit her lip. She hated to have Elizabeth

think of her as irresponsible. "Liz, I honestly don't know how I could have forgotten," she said. "To tell you the truth, I've just been so caught up in our painting workshop. . . ." Her voice trailed off, and Elizabeth just looked at her, as if she were waiting for Olivia to say something more. "I've never in my whole life met a man like Stuart before," Olivia gushed. "I think it's just knocked me off my feet a little."

Elizabeth regarded her with surprise and concern. "Olivia—" she began.

But Olivia cut her short. "I'd better go," she said, brushing her hair out of her eyes. "Liz, I promise I'll straighten the whole thing out with Penny and Mr. Collins. And I'll see you this afternoon—in painting workshop!"

She knew she really ought to go see Mr. Collins right then and there with Elizabeth. But Olivia didn't care. All she could think about was Stuart.

"So, I guess I owe you an apology," Elizabeth said to Enid later that afternoon. The girls had just finished their gym class and were walking together to their workshop. They were deep in discussion about Olivia and Mr. Bachman. "Olivia more or less admitted to me that she has a crush on Stuart. You should have seen how flustered and upset she was!" Elizabeth sighed. "And I've been insisting that *you* were making it all up!"

"Well, that's because you're the world's greatest friend, Elizabeth. You always give people the benefit of the doubt." She pushed a lock of curly hair behind her ear. "Let's both keep an eye on Olivia during class today and compare notes afterward. It's hard to tell yet if it's just a small crush or a full-blown disaster."

Elizabeth didn't answer for a minute. "I don't think Stuart realizes that Olivia has a crush on him. I think he just assumes she's really into painting and wants to learn everything she can."

"That makes sense," Enid said. "But it's turning into a real problem."

The two girls walked into the art room together. Olivia was already in the front of the room, talking earnestly to Mr. Bachman. Everyone else was setting up materials to begin work.

"Hi, you guys," Maria Santelli said. "You ready to start painting?"

"Yeah," Caroline Pearce said, overhearing. "But who can get a minute of Stuart's attention with Olivia monopolizing him all the time."

"I know what you mean," Maria said.

Elizabeth and Enid looked at each other. So the others in the class had noticed what was going on, too.

"It isn't Stuart's fault," Caroline added in an annoyed tone. "He's perfectly nice to everybody. It's just that Olivia doesn't give him a chance to help anyone else."

Elizabeth felt she had to defend her friend. "She's excited about painting, that's all," she said. But none of the other girls seemed to believe her. Elizabeth watched Olivia closely for the rest of the period, and she had to admit that what Caroline said was true. Wherever Stuart was, Olivia was right beside him. She volunteered to wash out brushes, to get more paint, to wipe up the floor, to help him put away the easels at the end of the class. She was behaving like a model student, volunteering for even the most disagreeable tasks with sincere enthusiasm.

Watching her, Elizabeth could honestly tell that the teacher might not see anything alarming in Olivia's behavior. After all, it was clear that Olivia was the one in the class who had the most talent. Already, even after just a few days, Olivia's work showed promise equaled by none of the others. So didn't it make sense that Olivia should be the one who was most eager to get Stuart's advice, to seek him out, to try to get as involved in the workshop as possible?

That was the way Elizabeth imagined it must seem to Mr. Bachman. He was too easygoing with them all to worry about how much attention one particular student was paying him.

But as Elizabeth watched her now, Olivia seemed obsessed. She barely acknowledged that she had discovered a new talent. She brushed off comments about her work and seemed to pay attention only when Mr. Bachman was talking or when someone was talking about him.

Even when she worked alone during the class, she brought his name up as often as she could. "Do you think I should add some blue here?" she asked Elizabeth. "Stuart says I should." Or, "Stuart doesn't like borders, so I thought I'd just leave this the way it is. . . ."

Elizabeth didn't even need to ask Enid what she thought when the bell rang and the workshop was over. One look at her friend's face told her all she wanted to know: Enid thought Olivia was in bad shape, too.

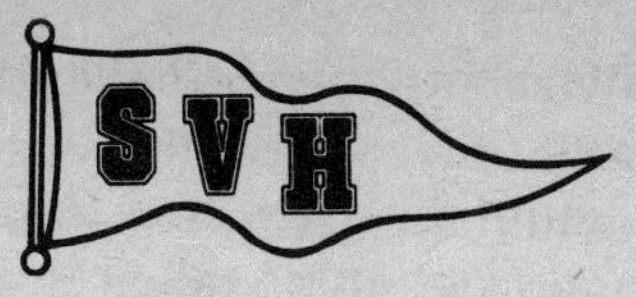

Six

"Did Lila tell you what her father and Anika Hunt are doing this weekend?" Amy Sutton asked Jessica. The two girls were standing at Jessica's locker on Friday morning. Amy had been chattering on and on, with Jessica only partly paying attention. Today marked the end of the first week of workshops, and she still didn't have an idea for a project.

"Yeah," Jessica muttered, jamming her hands deep into her pockets. "I heard all about it. Anika's taking him to the set of 'The Willoughbys.' And then they're going to hang out in Hollywood together and go to dinner at Ty Rourke's house." Ty Rourke was a hot new producer in Hollywood and *the* name in the entertainment world these days, according to Lila.

"I can't believe it." Amy sighed. "My mom's a broadcaster, but I've never gotten to meet any real stars. I wish I were Lila."

Jessica regarded Amy disdainfully. "I think Lila's making half this stuff up. How do we know for sure that her dad and Anika Hunt have even *met*, let alone fallen in love?"

Amy stared at her, her gray eyes wide. "What are you saying? You think Lila's making all this up? No way, Jess," she added reproachfully. "She's been way too specific about the whole thing. I mean, if you were going to invent some big story, you wouldn't bother to give all the little details. She might've said her father was seeing Anika Hunt again, but she wouldn't have told us all about Ty Rourke's party and that sort of thing. It would be too easy for us to check out."

"Now, Amy," Jessica said calmly, "that is exactly where you're wrong. Don't you know anything about the psychology of lying? For one thing, once you start telling one lie, the others just multiply."

"I don't know, Jess. I don't think you're right about Lila," she said.

Jessica was warming to the idea. "Come on, Amy. A really good lie is always specific. Like if some guy calls you up and asks you out and you don't want to go. If you just sort of vaguely say you're busy, he'll know you're lying. What if Randy Mason were to ask me out?" she offered as an example. "I'd say something like, 'Randy, I'd love to, but it so happens that Amy has invited me to watch videos of her family's trip to the Azores.' "

Amy giggled. "Why would you turn him down? I think you and Randy make a sweet couple."

Jessica rolled her eyes. "See what I mean about Lila? The main point is, she's refused to invite us to her house when Anika Hunt is supposedly there. Why would she do that if Anika really existed? It's obvious, Amy. The fact that she's given us so many little details about Anika Hunt makes the whole thing more suspect."

Amy narrowed her eyes. "Since when did you get to be such an expert, Jess? I don't see why Lila would want to lie about her father's love life."

"Don't you see?" Jessica cried. "She's trying to torture us by proving once again how ultra-glamorous her life is compared with our totally ordinary lives." She glared at Amy. "I think it's perfectly clear she's lying. I just wish I could prove it."

Amy shrugged. "Well, good luck," she said blithely. "What have you got in mind, putting her through the Inquisition?"

Jessica stared at Amy. "I've got it," she whispered, her eyes beginning to sparkle. "Amy, you just gave me the most wonderful idea for a project to make in my workshop!"

"What?" Amy demanded.

"A lie detector!" Jessica cried. "It's absolutely perfect! Then we can hook Lila right up to it and find out once and for all whether or not she's telling the truth about her father and Anika Hunt!"

Toward the end of the painting workshop, Friday afternoon, Stuart Bachman made an announcement. "Hard as it is to believe, we're halfway through with our class," he told them. "Next Friday you'll all be presenting your work in the auditorium. I just wanted to remind you that this weekend is going to be a very important time for you to do some work on your own. You might want to arrange to come in and work on Saturday or Sunday. I've set it up so that you'll be able to get into the school if you want. But in any case, at least devote some serious thought to your work over the weekend."

Olivia looked at Mr. Bachman with total devotion. Privately she was dreading the weekend, since she wouldn't be able to see him for two whole days. Everyone else was busy putting final touches on their work or starting to clean up, and Olivia took a minute to stroll up to his desk.

"Stuart," she said, shyly fiddling with a paintbrush, "I'm not feeling so great about my progress with my painting right now. Do you have any suggestions? I feel I need to get past the point I'm at, but I don't know how."

Stuart looked at her, and her heart beat rapidly. She loved the way he gazed intently into her eyes. He really seemed to listen and to take her seriously. "Well, sometimes when I feel stuck, I go to the museum and look at paintings by artists I really like. Why don't you try that this weekend?"

Olivia looked down, still fiddling with the brush. *Why can't I go to the museum with you?* she wanted to blurt out. But of course she would never say that, not in a million years. Just then her eye fell on a flier lying on the desk. It was an announcement about an alumni presentation at the Riverside Art Academy on Monday afternoon. Three speakers would be featured, the flier said. And one of them was Stuart.

"You're really going to be talking to the students there?" Olivia said eagerly.

"Yeah, but it isn't a very big deal. I'm just going to say a little about working to support painting after school ends." He studied the flier. "It's kind of fun, though—I did it last year, too." He looked curiously at Olivia. "Are you interested in coming along? You're pretty serious about art and art school, aren't you? It might be good for you to meet some people who are at Riverside." He tossed the flier back on the desk. "It's this Monday. Let me know if you'd like to come. I'd be happy to take you with me."

Olivia's eyes shone. She couldn't believe her ears. Stuart had asked her to come with *him* to an alumni meeting of his old art school! There was no denying what that meant.

She could barely meet his eyes. "I'd love to come," she choked out.

"Fine," Stuart said with a casual smile. "Remind me on Monday."

Olivia's ears were buzzing. She felt almost dizzy as she turned back to look at her painting. The colors swam together, and for a moment she could barely remember where she was.

She had never felt anything this intense before in her whole life. Stuart Bachman was literally all she could think about, and the most amazing thing of all was that he seemed to like her back!

Olivia was in such a reverie that she bumped into Elizabeth, who was carrying a jug of dirty water over to the sink. "Oops!" Olivia cried, blushing. "Sorry," she added, dabbing quickly at the water that had splashed onto Elizabeth's arm. "Sorry, Liz. I just didn't see where I was going!"

Elizabeth gave her a wry smile. "Never mind, Olivia," she said. "It's only water."

Olivia reddened under her friend's intense gaze. She felt funny about the look Elizabeth was giving her. So what if she was a little preoccupied? She was madly, head-over-heels in love, and she couldn't help the way she was behaving.

Well, it would all be fine, she assured herself. Next week Stuart was going to take her to the Riverside Alumni Day with him, and then the workshop would end and they could get involved without anybody caring. Only one more week to endure, and Stuart would be able to tell her exactly how he felt about her—that he was every bit as much in love with her as she was with him!

"Olivia," Mrs. Davidson said on Saturday morning, "do you realize you haven't said one word about what you want to do on your birthday?"

Olivia was trying to read the newspaper, but she was having a hard time concentrating. All she could think about was Stuart, and she just didn't see how she could possibly get through the entire weekend without seeing him.

"Don't you want to plan something special?" her mother asked.

Olivia shrugged. "Not really, Mom. Just having dinner with you and Daddy sounds perfect to me." An image flashed through her mind: She was sitting in an elegant restaurant, sipping champagne with Stuart. Next Friday the workshop would end. Maybe Stuart would ask her to go somewhere after the show in the auditorium.

"Well," her mother said, "then, if you don't mind, you'll let Daddy and me plan it?"

"Sure, Mom," Olivia said, sounding distracted. She pushed the paper to one side. "I've got to get moving. I want to pick up some supplies for the painting I'm working on."

Her mother nodded, and Olivia ran upstairs to change. Her heart was pounding because she knew she wasn't just going to the art supply store. She was going to drive past Stuart's apartment, too.

Twenty minutes later Olivia had parked her green van across from the small apartment building where Stuart lived. From the outside Olivia couldn't tell much. But she saw Stuart's car parked in the lot next to the building, and her heartbeat quickened. He was at home!

She peered up at the building, wondering which apartment was his. All of a sudden she had an overwhelming desire to see his place. "I can't just drop by without calling him. I need an excuse," she muttered, drumming her fingers on the dashboard.

Then she remembered what Stuart had told her the day before in class. Suppose she told him she couldn't find the painting she wanted to look at for inspiration in the museum and wanted to borrow one of his art books?

The minute the idea came to her, Olivia was out of the car, hurrying toward the building. She didn't stop to ask herself whether or not it was a good idea. All she knew was she *had* to see Stuart.

There were ten names listed on the directory in the lobby. Bachman was on the second floor. Number 214. Olivia dialed the number on the lobby phone, and after several rings Stuart answered. He sounded sleepy.

"Stuart?" she asked.

Stuart mumbled something, then coughed. "Hello? Who is it?"

"Stuart, it's Olivia. From your class," Olivia said. She felt panicked then. Was she out of her mind, just dropping by like this?

"Olivia? What time is it?" Stuart sounded really out of it. "I'm sorry, I'm still half asleep. I never get up before noon on weekends because I work really late at night."

Olivia's spirits lifted at once. He couldn't be in love with anyone if he spent weekend nights working, could he? "I'm sorry," she said quickly. "It's only ten-thirty, but I was out running some errands, and I remembered that I wanted to find a certain Hockney painting and it wasn't at the museum and I wondered if you had any books I could borrow." She said this all in a rush.

There was a long silence. Olivia wished she had never gone to Stuart's apartment house. Then Stuart said, "Look, give me a few minutes to get dressed. Then you can come up and have some coffee."

Olivia felt a surge of joy go through her. He didn't think she was nuts for coming over! He liked her! She had to hold herself down to keep from dancing around the lobby.

Five minutes later Stuart came down to let her in. He looked fantastic, his dark hair a little disheveled and his shirt untucked over a pair of worn jeans. He had his shirt-sleeves rolled up, and his arms looked sturdy and strong. "Hi," he said, smiling at her. "This is a real surprise. I don't think I've ever had a student as serious about painting as you, Olivia. You make me feel it's worthwhile being a teacher."

Olivia glowed. She didn't think she had ever been as happy in her whole life as she was right then. As she followed him up the stairs to his apartment, she said, "Well, I love your class."

"Good," he said, opening the door to his apartment and showing her in. "And I'm glad you stopped by, Olivia. I didn't mean to sound so confused. I'm really a late-night person. But you're welcome to look at my books and take whatever you need home with you."

Olivia felt shy as she glanced around. "What a wonderful place," she breathed. It was exactly the kind of apartment Olivia had always dreamed of—big and open, very spare, with just a few pieces of furniture and lots of windows. Everywhere she looked there were canvases, some finished, some not, some leaning against the walls, some on easels. "Can I look around?" she asked shyly.

"Sure," Stuart said, waving his hand. "Make

yourself at home. Do you want some coffee?" He disappeared into the kitchen, and Olivia glanced down at a photograph on the bookshelf. It was a photograph of Stuart with a couple of friends—one a woman about his age, very pretty, who was laughing.

"No, thanks," Olivia called back. She sat down on one of Stuart's chairs, waiting for him to come back and looking around her with fascination. She could hardly believe she was actually there.

When Stuart came back out, he had a coffeepot in one hand and two cups in the other. He poured her some, as if he hadn't heard her say no, and Olivia felt obliged to sip some. It tasted bitter, but she told him she liked it.

"I was up late last night working on something special," Stuart said, smiling at her. "Tell me what you think of these," he added, showing her some sketches for a pair of earrings.

"They're great," Olivia said admiringly.

"Really? You really like them?" Stuart asked. "I want to know because they're for a special occasion. I haven't shown the design to anyone yet. You're the first. You think a—" He broke off. "You like them? You'd wear them?"

Olivia nodded. "Oh, yeah. They're really fantastic."

"Good." He smiled at her, and Olivia felt tingly all over. Suddenly she had a wild thought. Somehow Stuart must have found out about her birthday, and the earrings were for her. No, that was impossible. But she couldn't shake the thought.

"All right," Stuart said, setting down his coffee cup. "Now, let's talk about Hockney and about your painting. Olivia, as I've told you before, I think you're talented. I'd like you to promise me that you'll put as much of yourself as you can into your art for the next few years because I think you've really got something."

Olivia stared at him. Was he just saying this because he liked her?

"Thank you," she said, feeling embarrassed. Olivia wasn't used to being complimented, and it made her feel uncomfortable to have someone as important as Stuart telling her to take her art seriously.

For the next half hour, she and Stuart talked about art, about inspiration, about where the good teachers were. Olivia listened carefully to every word Stuart said, knowing she would never forget their conversation. Then, before she left, Stuart sat beside her, and together they looked through his Hockney books.

By the time she left she could hardly wait to get back to work on her painting. She wanted it to be absolutely perfect—for Stuart.

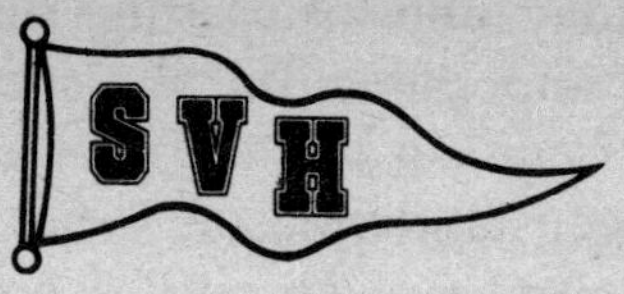

Seven

Jessica was sitting in the library during lunch hour on Monday, an encyclopedia open on her lap and a deep frown on her face. She had already devoted an entire half of lunch period to researching lie detectors, and she was no closer to figuring out how she was going to make one in the next five days.

She looked around the library and sighed. She couldn't imagine coming in here and working every day instead of hanging around with friends in the lunchroom. The thought made her shudder. But there were students who actually used the lunch hour to study. Jessica did a quick survey of who was in the library and smiled broadly when she saw Randy Mason hunched over an enormous book in one of the comfortable reading chairs in the center of the room.

Jessica looked at him for a long moment. Then,

encyclopedia under one arm, she got up and strolled in his direction. She waited until she was practically on top of him before stopping and saying, "Randy Mason! What are you doing stuck in the library on such a gorgeous sunny day?"

Randy looked up and nervously adjusted his glasses. "Uh, hi, Jessica," he stammered. "I'm just doing some, uh, extra reading."

Jessica pushed her silky hair back and forced herself to look down at Randy with an expression of sweet admiration. "Boy, I wish I could be like you," she said.

Randy stared at her. "You do? Why?"

Good question, Jessica thought. "Uh, because you're so good at science and stuff. You really understand the project you're doing in our workshop." *That was inspired,* Jessica praised herself. She had managed to get right to the point. She lowered her eyes. "While poor me . . ." she added sorrowfully. "I've finally figured out the best thing to make, only I don't have the faintest idea how."

Randy blinked. "What do you want to make? Maybe I can help you," he said.

Jessica was delighted. Those were exactly the words she had hoped to hear. The next minute she had plopped down next to Randy, opened the book to *lie detectors,* and told him all about her idea.

Randy blinked again. "That doesn't sound

very hard. All you need is a blood pressure detection device and a device to transmit the information."

Jessica stared at him. "Right," she said uneasily. "That's sort of what I thought. Like, maybe taking a garage door opener and attaching it to something you could put on your index finger, or—"

Randy covered his mouth with his hand and let out a noise somewhere between a grunt and a giggle.

"What is it?" Jessica demanded.

"Nothing." He took his hand away from his mouth. "Why don't you let me make a few suggestions?"

Jessica couldn't think of any words she would rather have heard. For the next half hour, she sat beaming at Randy Mason as he ignored his own work and concentrated on hers.

By the end of lunch hour she was absolutely confident that the lie detector was going to work. She breezed out into the hallway, a big smile on her face, and didn't even mind when Lila caught up with her and started droning on and on about her father and his latest date with Anika Hunt.

"That's great," Jessica said coolly. "But maybe you shouldn't tell so many people about your father and Anika, Lila."

"Why?" Lila demanded.

Jessica shrugged. "Oh, you know how it is.

You wouldn't want to be embarrassed if someone just happened to prove that you, you know, had sort of exaggerated the facts a little bit."

Lila stared at her indignantly. "Jessica, how can you say something like that?" she cried.

Jessica raised her eyebrows. "Don't get defensive, Lila," she said sweetly. "For heaven's sake. If you're telling the complete and utter truth, what on earth have you got to worry about?"

And before Lila could say a word in response, Jessica sailed down the hall. *Thank heavens,* she thought blissfully, *for Randy Mason!*

"I can't believe we only have one school week left to get our projects ready," Elizabeth said at lunchtime.

Enid was the only one at the table who seemed to respond to what she had said. Olivia was deep in a book on Hockney's painting techniques, and Jeffrey was reading a computer manual.

Enid giggled. "It looks like this table is pretty good proof that everyone's working hard," she said. Neither Jeffrey nor Olivia responded to this comment, and she tried again. "Hey, haven't you two heard that it's rude to read during meals?"

Jeffrey put down his manual and smiled apologetically. "I'm sorry. It's just that this game is turning out to be harder to write than I expected."

"I think a lot of us are finding out something like that," Elizabeth said, then sighed. "I've got tons of work to do on my painting before Friday. Hey, have you guys heard about Lila's dress?" she asked, breaking into a giggle.

Enid and Jeffrey shook their heads. Olivia, beside them, was still intent on her book. She seemed to be in another world.

"Well, apparently Lila sewed the darts in backward by mistake. Cara told me that she's really upset, saying she won't be caught dead in it. And she doesn't seem to think there's time to fix it, either." Elizabeth giggled again. "Can you imagine Lila wearing a dress with the darts sewn inside out?"

Enid started cracking up, too. "This Friday is going to be great. I can't wait to see what everyone's come up with over the past couple of weeks." She paused for a second. "Like your sister, for instance. Has Jessica managed to make an electronic something-or-other yet?"

Elizabeth shook her head. "Not that I know of. But last night she was all mysterious about it, muttering that she'd figured out something that was pure genius."

Jeffrey laughed. "Well, she must have come up with it outside of class, then, because so far she hasn't done much in the workshop but look miserable."

Elizabeth was staring at Olivia curiously. "Hey, Olivia, I knew there was something going on this Friday other than the show in the auditorium. Isn't it your birthday?"

Olivia put down her book. "That's right," she said casually.

Elizabeth smiled at her. "So, what have you got lined up, Liv? Are you going to have a party?"

Olivia shook her head. "Oh, no. I don't really feel like making a big deal out of it."

Elizabeth and Enid looked at each other, and Elizabeth cleared her throat. "But you can't just have a birthday and not even celebrate," she insisted.

"Yeah," Enid agreed. "Why don't we all have dinner over at my house?"

Olivia raised her eyebrows. "Thanks, Enid. It's nice of you to invite me, but I don't know. I'm sure I'll end up doing something special," she said lightly. She paused for a minute, then leaned forward, as if she were about to confide in her friends. "There's only one thing I'd really like to do to celebrate, anyway. And I think it's going to happen."

Enid kicked Elizabeth under the table as Olivia got to her feet, then picked up the Hockney book as if it were made of gold. "This is Stuart's book," she said rapturously. "I'd better go find him so I can give it back to him." With that she sailed off, clutching the enormous book to her chest.

Enid gave Elizabeth a look. "Pretty serious,"

she muttered. "Did that mean what I think it meant? That all Olivia wants for her birthday is to spend time with Stuart Bachman?"

Jeffrey looked confused. "I don't get it. Isn't he way too old for her?" he asked.

Elizabeth patted him soothingly on the hand. "Don't worry," she assured him. "It's not going to turn into an epidemic around here."

"But Stuart is pretty cute," Enid reminded them. "And to tell you the truth, I think he's interested in Olivia. I don't think she's just imagining things."

Elizabeth's eyes widened. "No way," she protested. "Stuart is nice to Olivia the same way he's nice to everyone. Olivia has a gigantic crush on him, that's for sure. But I don't think for one single second that he feels anything back for her."

Enid shrugged. "Well, I can't prove it, but just do me a favor and watch him today in workshop. Then tell me you think Stuart Bachman isn't leading Olivia on!"

Enid and Elizabeth made sure to set their easels up right next to each other that afternoon so they could share opinions on everything they saw going on between Olivia and the art teacher.

Olivia was early, as always. By the time the rest of the students arrived, she was already helping Stuart by distributing materials. She spent most of the hour working right near Stuart's desk. All of this was standard. But today Elizabeth was concentrating on Stuart.

She couldn't help agreeing with Enid that Stuart's behavior was peculiar. He looked at Olivia whenever he made announcements. He came over and checked her work dozens of times. It really seemed as if everyone else in the class was just there as a backdrop, and that Olivia was the only one who mattered.

"I just think it's because Olivia has the most talent," Elizabeth whispered to her friend. "It's a case of favoritism, but nothing more."

"Yeah?" Enid whispered back. "What about the way he's looking at her now?"

It was true. Stuart had a different expression on his face when he looked at Olivia. He was staring at the painting on her easel, a look of admiration and fascination in his eyes. Then he turned to Olivia, and the look he gave her was intense. "I want to talk to you about this later," he said.

Enid poked Elizabeth. "See?"

"Wait a second," Elizabeth said, pretending to lean over to retrieve some brushes so she could hear what Stuart was saying next. His voice was low, and she had to strain to make out the words.

"Are we still on for this afternoon? You're sure you really want to go?" Stuart asked.

Olivia nodded emphatically. "I definitely want to. Where should we meet?"

"Well," Stuart said, glancing down at his watch, "how about if I meet you at my car at four o'clock. We have a meeting here after school for about forty-five minutes, and I have a few phone calls to make."

"Four o'clock is fine," Olivia said.

Elizabeth's eyes widened. This was serious. Olivia and Stuart were actually making plans to meet outside of school!

"I think we should say something to her," Enid said heatedly as she and Elizabeth turned back to their work.

Elizabeth shook her head. "I don't want to butt in," she said uneasily. "Look, Enid, I'm sure Olivia knows what she's doing."

But for the first time, Elizabeth wondered whether or not that was really the case. She didn't like the sound of the conversation she had just overheard. One thing was certain: Olivia and Stuart's friendship had progressed beyond that of teacher and student. Where were they going together? Was Olivia getting into something she wouldn't be able to handle?

Elizabeth could see why Enid felt tempted to intervene. But she didn't think it was up to them to approach Olivia. All they could do was be around for her if she decided to ask for advice. In the meantime, they had to hope that Olivia and Stuart knew what they were doing.

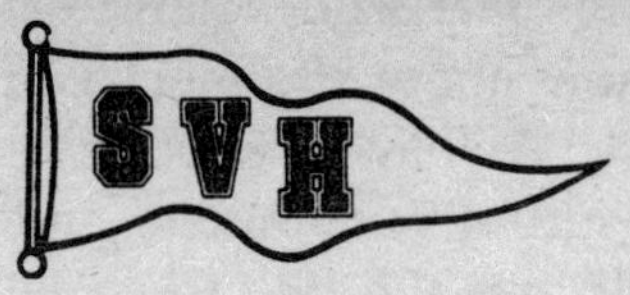

Eight

Olivia checked her appearance nervously in the ladies' room on the first floor of the Riverside Art Academy. She couldn't believe she was here with Stuart. The school was absolutely wonderful. Only about sixty students were admitted at any one time, and Stuart had taken her around on a complete tour to show her the studios and the special rooms for student exhibitions. He had also introduced her to students and teachers as one of his prize students, which made her glow with pride.

"Where's Monica?" one of the teachers asked Stuart while he was glancing over his notes for his speech.

"She's in L.A. for a few days," Stuart said.

Olivia was burning with curiosity as she moved away from him to look at a painting. Who was Monica? But the next minute she forgot all about it when Stuart called her over to be introduced to a group of teachers. Whoever Monica was, she was out of town—far away. Olivia was right here, being introduced to people as a future artist, as Stuart's prize pupil!

After about half an hour of socializing it was time for the speakers. Olivia sat right in the front row, gazing proudly at Stuart while he gave his talk. He was so poised, so witty. Every time he made a joke and the audience laughed, Olivia felt her heart soar. His talk was brief but wonderful and inspiring. He talked about how artists could earn a living doing what they loved. "All of you can be artists. Remember that," Stuart concluded to a rousing burst of applause. Olivia clapped harder than anyone else. She thought she would faint with joy when Stuart came and sat next to her for the other two speeches. Every time he leaned closer to her to whisper something, her heart thumped like crazy. All in all, it was one of the best afternoons she could remember. She couldn't help feeling disappointed when, by five-thirty, people were putting on their jackets and slipping away. But her mood soared when Stuart asked, "Do you have to get home right away? I'd love to ask you to do me a big favor if you don't."

"Oh, no. I don't have to be home until six-thirty," Olivia said, instantly regretting that she made it sound as though she had a curfew to meet. She thought of Stuart's wonderful apartment. He could do whatever he liked, whenever he felt like it. And for just a second the number of years between them seemed immense.

But Stuart didn't seem to have noticed her discomfort. "Great! Would you be an angel and come with me to this great store called Domain? I'm looking for a present for a very special friend, and I'm having a hard time deciding what's right. Want to help me out? I trust your taste, Olivia." He winked at her, and Olivia felt her face glow with warmth.

She remembered the earrings Stuart was designing. And again, she couldn't help thinking he had found out about her birthday somehow. Maybe the earrings were for someone else. But asking her to come with him to help pick out a present for "a special friend"—that person had to be her!

Ten minutes later they were parked outside the sleek ultramodern store. "I love this place. If I could afford it, I'd get all sorts of stuff from here for my apartment," Stuart said, hopping out of his car. "Unfortunately, like most artists, I'm lucky to be able to pay my rent each month." He grinned at her. "But I'm splurging on this present. So I want to know what you think."

Olivia swallowed and nodded. She wished she could tell Stuart not to spend his money. But how could she, when he hadn't definitely said he was buying something for her? She followed him into the store, feeling, as she had felt at the lecture, the thrill of going anywhere with him. He had such incredible presence. All the salespeople looked at him with interest as he wandered around, eyeing the expensive items in the store.

Olivia had never been in a store like it before. The lamps cost more than she could believe! There were lots of expensive, strange-looking trinkets. Stuart was turning a silver goblet over in his hand, frowning. Each object he picked up he set down again with a look of disappointment.

Olivia stopped short in front of a lovely picture frame made of light wood with darker wood inlaid in a geometric pattern. "This is pretty," she said softly.

"What is it?" Stuart came over to take a look. "Olivia, you're a genius! This is great!" he cried, picking up the frame. Then he set it down. "Well, oh, I don't know." He sighed. "I'm going to have to think it over," he said apologetically to the salesgirl hovering near them. "I'm looking for a present for a friend. It's a special occasion, and the gift has to be just perfect."

"I understand," the saleswoman said with a smile. She looked quizzically at Olivia, who blushed under her scrutiny. She wasn't used to being stared at the way people seemed to stare at Stuart.

She wondered if the saleswoman wished she were the one Stuart was buying presents for. Olivia didn't blame her if that was true. She felt embarrassed as she followed Stuart out to his car. "A special occasion . . ." Was that supposed to be her birthday? How on earth had he found out about it? Had someone at school mentioned it by accident?

"So, what's this special thing coming up, Stuart?" she asked casually while they were driving home.

Stuart shrugged. "Nothing. Don't give it a thought." He winked at her again, and Olivia felt her heartbeat speed up for the thousandth time that day.

She was positive it was her birthday he was thinking of, absolutely positive. She just hoped whatever surprise Stuart was planning wasn't going to interfere with anything her parents had set up for Friday.

"Hi, sweetie," Mrs. Davidson said when Olivia came hurrying in a few minutes later. "How was your day?"

"Fine," Olivia said, giving her a quick hug. "Mom? Would it be OK if I set up my easel in the basement for the next few days? I really want to work hard on my painting for Stuart's class, and I don't think there's enough time at school."

"Sure." Mrs. Davidson smiled at her. "I'm glad to see that you're so devoted to painting, Olivia. Did you know that Grandmother Lea was a serious oil painter?"

"You're kidding!" Olivia was surprised. She

had never known her maternal grandmother, who had died before Olivia was born. "Wow. Was she good?"

"We have some of her paintings in the attic. I think she was good," her mother continued calmly. "But she never really got the training or support she needed. You know, in those days it was harder for women to break away from traditional roles. She ended up spending most of her time raising her family."

Olivia nodded thoughtfully. "I'd love to see some of her paintings," she said. Deep in thought, she slipped out of her jacket. She was wondering whether or not she would care as much about painting if Stuart wasn't her teacher. Was she really devoted to art, or was it the idea of pleasing him that mattered most?

For the next hour Olivia sat downstairs in the finished basement, making sketch after sketch. Tomorrow she would have to bring her canvas home from school so she could work on it at length. Right now she just wanted to experiment with different shapes. Olivia lost all track of time. She couldn't believe an hour had elapsed when her mother called her upstairs for dinner.

"Someone called while you were working, but I didn't want to disturb you," her mother said.

Stuart! Olivia thought, her heart racing. "Who was it?" she demanded.

"Someone named Rod. He said he's in your

English class," her mother said. "He sounded very nice."

Olivia wrinkled her brow. "Rod . . . Sullivan," she said at last. "I wonder why he's calling me? I barely know him."

"Maybe he wants to get to know you better," her mother suggested.

Olivia shrugged. Rod Sullivan hadn't ever made an impression on her one way or another. He seemed like a perfectly nice guy, but no one to get excited about. Not like Stuart.

Tuesday morning Olivia was at school almost an hour early. She wanted to work on her painting before first-period class began. It was an ideal time to paint, she found. The school was deserted and quiet, and she felt that she made real progress.

She was thinking hard about Stuart as she walked to her first-period class, and she barely noticed Rod Sullivan hurrying to catch up with her. "Olivia!" he gasped. "Can I talk to you for a second?"

Olivia turned to him, a quizzical expression on her face. "My mom said you called last night," she said.

"Yeah, I did. I got your name from Mr. Collins. I have some ideas for changing the graphics and typesetting of the school paper, and he said I should show them to you, since you're the arts editor. Can we get together sometime soon? I'd really like to know what you think of my stuff."

Olivia looked at him more closely. He was nice-looking, on the thin side, with light brown hair and tortoiseshell glasses. "Sure, Rod. I'm pretty busy this week, though. I'm trying to get a painting finished for the show on Friday."

Rod nodded. "I've been working on graphics and layout in my workshop—the printing one. That's how I got so caught up in it. And I've found I really like doing the work. I think the school paper could really use a new look," he added.

"Well, can we wait till next week?" Olivia asked.

"Sure." Rod gave her a warm smile. "By the way, I really like the stuff you print in the paper. I think you're an excellent editor."

Olivia smiled back. He was a nice guy. She wondered why she had never noticed him before.

"Look," he said suddenly, blushing a little, "why don't we get together sometime this week-end? Like, do something fun, go see a movie or something?"

Olivia stared at him. Was he asking her out on a date? She was shocked. "Oh, uh, well, thanks, Rod, but . . ." But what? She didn't really have an excuse. She just stared at him, embarrassed, until he backed off, his face crimson.

"Never mind," he murmured.

He turned and fled, leaving Olivia staring after him and feeling like a jerk.

Then Stuart came up behind her, his arms full of supplies. "Hi, Olivia," he said, giving her a big smile. He looked down the hall after Rod. "You sure seem to have scared him off! Is anything wrong?"

Olivia shook her head. "No. I was just surprised, that's all. He, uh, kind of asked me out, and I barely know him."

Stuart smiled broadly. "He has good taste," he said, patting her on the arm. "I bet you break hearts around this place all the time."

Olivia didn't answer. She fell in step beside Stuart. "Did you decide about the picture frame?" she asked casually.

Stuart shook his head. "No, not yet. I've still got some time left, though. But thanks again for your help, Olivia. I really appreciate it."

Olivia nodded. She paused, leaving Stuart a perfect opportunity to say something more about Friday, but he didn't. "I'd better run with these things," he said. "See you later in class."

Olivia sighed and nodded. Well, she was just going to have to wait until Friday to find out what the surprise was going to be.

* * *

That day Olivia joined Elizabeth and Enid for a quick lunch. "I'm trying to hurry so I can get some extra work in on my painting," she told them, eating her sandwich in a few hurried bites.

Elizabeth nodded. "That sounds like a good idea. I need to do more work, too."

She looked closely at Olivia. "By the way, I think you have a new fan. Rod Sullivan was asking me tons of questions about you yesterday."

Olivia brushed a strand of hair off her forehead. "Yeah, I ran into him today. He wants to change the graphics of the paper. Do you think that people would like something new?"

Elizabeth nodded. "Definitely. I think he's got some good ideas, and he seems like a really nice guy," she said casually, watching her friend's reaction.

Olivia shrugged. "Yeah, he seems OK," she said.

"Hey," Enid said, remembering, "you sure you don't want to come over and have a birthday dinner at my house on Friday night, Olivia?"

Olivia shook her head with a smile. "To tell you the truth, I have the distinct impression a friend is planning something for that night." She blushed and stared at the table, but she couldn't stand it. She had to tell them. "I think Stuart's going to surprise me. But don't tell anyone."

Enid looked at her with surprise. "Really? What makes you think so?"

Olivia shrugged dreamily. "He's dropped some hints. You know how it is," she added. "You can just tell!"

Elizabeth glanced at her with alarm. At this point she didn't know which would be worse. Either Olivia had blown everything out of proportion and was counting on something that wasn't going to take place, or Stuart really *was* planning to surprise her for her birthday with some special celebration.

What exactly was going on between the art teacher and Olivia? Looking at Olivia in the cafeteria, Elizabeth felt a real twinge of concern. She hoped her friend knew what she was getting herself into!

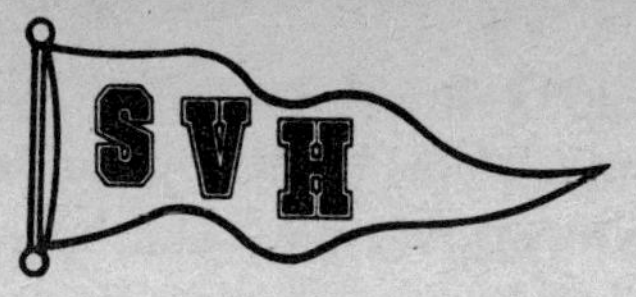

Nine

Jessica was fiddling with her lie detector in her room on Wednesday morning before breakfast. She had the door closed so no one could see what she was doing. She didn't want to spoil the debut of what she was convinced would be the greatest project to come out of any of the minicourses. She was just getting the device to work right when someone pounded on her door. Elizabeth came storming in before Jessica could even respond.

"What is it?" Jessica asked, stuffing the lie dectector into a drawer so Elizabeth couldn't see it.

"I want to know why you left my very good silk blouse lying on the floor of my closet," Elizabeth said, crossing her arms and glaring at her. "You said you'd take it to the cleaners if you borrowed it. So why is it there?"

Jessica looked distressed. "Whoops. I guess I kind of forgot. Sorry, Liz."

"Sorry isn't good enough," Elizabeth said. "How many times have I asked you to be more responsible about things you borrow?"

Jessica bit her lip. "Just give me one more chance, Lizzie. Don't be mad at me."

Elizabeth's eyes were flashing. "I'm really tempted to tell Mom about this," she muttered.

It wasn't characteristic of Elizabeth to take her problems elsewhere, but she was really angry.

Jessica looked indignant. "Come on, Liz. Don't tell on me. You know that isn't fair," she protested.

Elizabeth took a deep breath. "Maybe not. But it isn't fair taking something of mine and returning it without even having it cleaned." Before Jessica could say another word, Elizabeth stomped off, leaving her twin staring after her with concern.

Jessica felt terrible about the blouse. She just hoped Elizabeth didn't rat on her. How would she know? She would have to wait and see whether or not her mother yelled at her. But as she opened the drawer to retrieve the lie detector, she had an idea. She could actually try it out on Elizabeth, once she got it working. Maybe this little device was going to be useful for more than just a workshop project.

Wednesday morning Olivia spent longer than

usual dawdling over her breakfast. Her mother was engrossed in the paper, and Olivia found it hard to get her attention.

The truth was, she wanted to ask her mother's advice. Usually Olivia kept her private life to herself. But her feelings for Stuart were beginning to get out of hand, and she wanted to tell someone about them.

She had never experienced anything like this before in her whole life. She thought about Stuart all the time. She had started driving past his apartment to see whether or not his car was out front. She had looked up his phone number, and twice she had called his apartment from the pay phone in school, knowing he wouldn't be at home, just so she could hear how sexy his voice sounded on his answering machine.

Was this what falling in love was supposed to feel like?

"Mom," she said in a small voice.

Mrs. Davidson put down the paper. "What is it, sweetie? You look tired. Are you coming down with something?"

Olivia shook her head. She was thinking, *No, I've already got it, bad. A major case of madly-in-love.* "I'm fine, Mom. I was just thinking. If you really like someone, how can you tell—well, what if you *think* this person likes you back, but you're not really sure?"

Mrs. Davidson beamed at her. "Does this

have anything to do with that nice boy who called here the other day? What was his name—Rod?"

Rod? Olivia stared at her mother. "You mean Rod Sullivan?" she demanded. Rod Sullivan! She couldn't believe it. If her mother only knew. . . . "No, Mom," was all she said. "It's somebody else."

"Oh," her mother said, appearing confused. "Well, I don't know, darling. Do you think he likes you? Have you talked to him about it?"

Olivia shook her head. "Not yet. I've sort of been waiting for—for the appropriate moment."

"Well, I always think it's best to be straightforward about these things. There's no harm in telling him you like him, Liv. You're such a great girl. How could anyone you like not like you back?"

Olivia just stared at her. Sometimes mothers were amazingly uninformed about love. She could think of a million reasons why Stuart Bachman wouldn't be interested in her. A million and one. "Listen, Mom," she went on, changing the subject, "about my birthday . . ."

Mrs. Davidson picked the paper up again. "Oh, don't worry, dear. Your father and I took you at your word. We talked it over, and we decided if you really didn't want to make a fuss, we wouldn't."

Olivia couldn't believe it. She had expected her mother to put up a fight. "You mean you haven't planned anything?" she asked. Her first feeling was enormous relief. Now she could go ahead with Stuart and enjoy whatever surprise he had lined up.

But she couldn't help feeling a tiny pang of disappointment. She had always spent birthdays doing something fun with her parents. Was this a sign she was finally growing up? If so, she wasn't sure how thrilled she was. "Well," she said in a small voice, "I'm sure one or two of my friends will want to do something."

"I'm sure," Mrs. Davidson said matter-of-factly, absorbed in the paper.

Olivia felt her lower lip quiver just a little bit. She hoped Stuart really *was* planning something. Otherwise, this was going to be the saddest birthday ever!

Olivia wanted to get to painting class early that day. She still had quite a bit of work to do on her piece, and she wanted to get a head start. Stuart had made arrangements so that students who had study halls before class could use the extra time to paint, and Olivia was taking advantage of the free time.

She was almost at the door of the studio when Rod Sullivan called her name. "Olivia! Hi," he said, hurrying to catch up with her.

"Hi." She smiled at him. "How are you?"

"Good. I just wanted to show you something." He dug around in his backpack. "I did a special layout yesterday for you. I wanted you to take a look at it."

Olivia looked with interest at the layout Rod had designed. There was no denying he had talent. He had made interesting use of graphics around the borders, and the typesetting he'd recommended was much bolder and more interesting than what the newspaper currently used.

"Thanks, Rod. It looks really good," she said. "I'll show it to Mr. Collins and see what he thinks." He brushed her hand as she took the page from him, and she blushed slightly.

"Well, I just wanted to show you this. That's all," he said, looking awkward again. Then, before she could say another word, he blurted, "You want to go see a movie on Friday night?"

"Oh, I'm sorry, Rod, but I think I'm busy on Friday," Olivia said. She actually *did* feel sorry this time. Rod was really sweet. He would probably be fun to go out with. But she wasn't going to miss Stuart's surprise for anything!

"OK, well, some other time," Rod muttered, folding up the paper and hurrying off before Olivia could say anything else to him.

"Breaking hearts again?" a low voice behind her said. Olivia whirled around just as Stuart approached, a quizzical smile on his face.

"Hi, Stuart," she said, her heart pounding the way it always did whenever she saw him.

She couldn't help thinking how different it was talking to him than to a boy her own age, like Rod. Her conversations with Stuart about art and inspiration were so thrilling compared to most of the small talk she shared with her fellow students.

"How are you today?" Stuart asked, following Olivia into the art room. His arms were full of books and paper, and when he set everything down on the desk, Olivia saw a flier fall out onto the floor.

"I'll get it,' she said, bending over to pick it up. Her gaze fell on it, and her eyes widened with surprise. "New Paintings from Stuart Bachman," it said. "Preview: Friday the Twenty-second, Madison Gallery."

Friday the twenty-second? That was this Friday. Her birthday. If Stuart had an opening, that meant. . . . She blinked, trying to hide her disappointment. That meant he couldn't have been planning anything for her birthday after all.

"You're having an exhibit open?" she said, trying to make her voice sound neutral. She didn't want him to see how upset she was.

"Oh, yeah. That's for you. I want you to come," Stuart said casually. "I mean it," he added, looking closely at her. "There's going to be a kind of surprise there for you. Promise you'll come."

"A surprise?" Olivia repeated faintly.

Stuart nodded. "Promise you'll come," he said again. "It's very important."

Olivia stared at him, puzzled. She didn't know what to think. A surprise? Could that have anything to do with the special occasion he had mentioned the other day?

Suddenly her spirits soared. Of course! She had been a complete idiot about the whole thing. Obviously Stuart was planning to surprise her at the gallery. Maybe he had planned some kind of special present for her there. Or maybe—she barely dared to imagine this—he was going to give her a painting for her birthday!

She felt so happy she didn't think she could bear it. Everything seemed to click into place. Olivia looked deep into his eyes. "I promise. I'll be there, Stuart," she said softly.

"Good! Now, don't forget," he admonished. He followed her over to her easel, inspecting her painting with interest as she set it up. "It's looking great, Olivia. I'm really pleased with your progress."

"Thanks," she said, dropping her eyes.

But as good as it made her feel to know that Stuart liked her painting, the real thrill was thinking about Friday. Everything was going to be wonderful once they could finally build their relationship outside the classroom!

Elizabeth and Enid were upstairs in Elizabeth's bedroom, looking through a pile of magazines and catching up on gossip, when Jessica barged in, her eyes sparkling.

"I want to try something out on you two," she cried. "Enid, give me your hand and let me strap you to the very first Jessica Wakefield Lie-Detecting Device!"

Elizabeth and Enid stared at her. "What?" Elizabeth cried, watching with fascination as her sister slid Enid's second finger into a thimble attached to a long wire, which was in turn attached to a digital pulse gauge.

"Here's how it works. I take a reading of your pulse—the number represents how many times your pulse beats per minute. Everyone's resting rate is a little different." Jessica recorded Enid's pulse. "Yours is one-twenty over eighty, Enid. Perfect. Now I ask you a question, and you answer, keeping your finger in the little thimble. If you lie, your pulse should speed up. Otherwise, it should stay the same." She was clearly enjoying herself. "OK, Liz, what should we ask her?"

"Let's see." Elizabeth thought for a moment. Then with a twinkle in her eye, she asked, "Enid, did you take Liz's second piece of pizza today at lunch while she wasn't looking?"

"Nope," Enid said.

"See! It's working! Your pulse just sped up!" Jessica cried, overjoyed.

"That's amazing. I really *did* take the second piece of pizza," Enid said, looking impressed.

"Your turn," Jessica said to Elizabeth and went through the same procedure.

"Now," Jessica said after she had written down Elizabeth's pulse rate, "Liz, did you tell Mom about the blouse? Tell the truth."

Elizabeth glowered. "I should have. But I didn't," she grumbled. Jessica's eyes flew to the gauge. Sure enough, it stayed stable. Elizabeth seemed to be telling the truth.

"What a good sister," she said, patting Elizabeth's arm.

"Jess, how did you figure out how to make that thing?" Elizabeth asked skeptically.

Jessica smiled condescendingly. "I happen to know a thing or two about electronics, Liz. Don't look at me like you think I stole this from someone. Can I help it if I came up with the best project in the class?"

The phone rang, and Jessica dived for it, almost knocking her sister over in the process. "Oh, hi, Mrs. Davidson," she said. She listened for a minute, nodding once or twice. "Sure. That sounds great. Do you want to speak with my sister?" And she passed the phone to Elizabeth, saying, "Mrs. Davidson is having a surprise party for Olivia on Friday night. She wants us all there at eight sharp."

Elizabeth took the phone and thanked Mrs. Davidson. "I think that sounds like a great idea," she said warmly. But at the back of her mind a warning bell went off. Wasn't Olivia planning to do something with Stuart?

"Also, I wanted to ask you if you knew whether or not I should invite Rod Sullivan," Mrs. Davidson said. "He's called here a couple of times for Olivia, and he sounds like such a nice boy. But I'm not sure if Olivia would like that."

Elizabeth coughed and looked at Enid. "Oh, I think she would," she said. "Is there anything we can do to help you? Would you like us to bring something?"

"Just yourselves. Her father and I are taking care of everything. Just be here by eight. We want this to be a complete surprise."

Elizabeth nodded. "Fine," she said.

She had a feeling that the party was going to be a bigger surprise than Mrs. Davidson could possibly imagine. But Elizabeth was delighted it was going to take place. She had been worried about Olivia's birthday, and it made her feel much better knowing that something special was being planned.

It isn't wrong to have said to go ahead and invite Rod, she assured herself.

Still, Elizabeth had an uneasy feeling about Friday night. She just hoped everything turned out the way Mrs. Davidson planned.

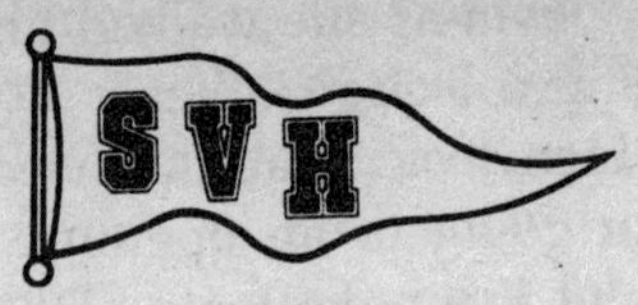

Ten

Olivia was so excited about the exhibition, she could barely keep it to herself. In fact, on Wednesday afternoon she impulsively decided to drive downtown after school to find something special to wear.

She wasn't sure what would be appropriate for an opening. Besides, she had no idea what kind of surprise Stuart had lined up for after the show. Olivia parked her van across the street from a little boutique called L'Idée, a brand-new store right next to Domain, where she and Stuart had looked at the picture frame.

This wasn't the kind of store Olivia normally shopped in. Usually she bought all of her soft cotton dresses at the same boutique. But she had gotten a check for her birthday from her grandmother that morning, and she felt like splurging.

"Can I help you?" the saleswoman asked,

looking at Olivia as she walked timidly around the expensive-looking clothes.

Olivia blurted out that she needed a special dress. "I'm going to an opening. And I want something to make me look, well, older. More sophisticated," she said.

The saleswoman regarded her shrewdly. "I've got just the thing," she said. A minute later she brought out a dark purple silk jumpsuit. It didn't seem like much on the hanger, but when Olivia put it on, she had to admit it was fabulous.

"This is great," she breathed, turning slowly in front of the mirror. She looked completely different—like a model in a magazine. The jumpsuit was so unlike her that she couldn't imagine daring to wear it in public.

"Now, wait a second. There's a scarf that goes with it, and a belt." The saleswoman deftly tied the silky scarf around Olivia's neck, then helped her fasten on a broad leather belt. The total effect was superb.

"I'll take it," Olivia said. "The whole thing." She couldn't believe she was doing this. First of all, she had never spent so much money on one outfit in her whole life. And second, would she really be brave enough to wear it on Friday?

"Be sure to wear some makeup, too," the saleswoman instructed her as she rang up the outfit. "You really want to make a *statement*."

Olivia hid a giggle. She would be making a

statement, all right! She just hoped she didn't scare away everyone at the opening!

She was still smiling to herself when she stepped outside a moment later, her package in her hand. She was just glancing to her right to check traffic before crossing the street when she saw Stuart opening the door to Domain.

Without stopping to think, Olivia ducked inside the boutique and waited for him to reappear. She kept checking outside, and finally, a few minutes later, he reemerged with a small package in his hands.

The picture frame!

Olivia was sure that he'd gone back and chosen it for her. Any doubts about Stuart's plan for her birthday completely vanished.

She hugged her package to her chest and smiled contentedly. This Friday was going to be spectacular. She didn't know what she was most looking forward to, the exhibition or the surprise Stuart had lined up for her afterward!

"Come on, you guys," Amy urged, giving Lila and Jessica her most impatient look. "I told you, I've got to be home by five to help my mom make dinner. I don't have all afternoon to poke around shops in the mall!"

"Lila, why didn't you design a dress like that?" Jessica asked, pointing to a sophisticated evening dress in the window of a shop. The three girls had intended to spend the afternoon buying a present for Olivia's birthday, but they kept getting distracted. Especially Lila, who stopped in front of every single boutique and stared raptly at the clothes on display.

"I wish Daddy would buy me a fur coat," Lila said with a sigh, ignoring Jessica's comment.

Jessica rolled her eyes. "He's probably saving up for a special present for Anika," she said sarcastically.

Lila looked at her with big hurt eyes. "Jess, I really don't see why you have to be so snide about my father and Anika Hunt. I think it's really nice Daddy finally has a steady girlfriend." She flipped her hair back over her shoulders. "Besides, have you even thought for a minute how hard it is on me, living alone with Daddy without a woman in the house? You ought to be happy for me!"

"Right," Jessica said sarcastically. Then she added. "Just wait. I'll show you on Friday how happy I am about the whole thing."

Lila gave her a blank look. "I don't really understand, Jessica. What does Friday have to do with Anika Hunt and my father?"

Jessica gave Amy a warning poke. "Nothing. It's a surprise," she said vaguely.

"Speaking of Friday," Amy said, changing the subject slightly, "how's your dress coming, Lila?"

"I don't want to talk about it," she muttered.

"It can't be that bad," Amy said soothingly.

Lila looked miserable. "I told you I sewed the darts inside out, right?"

Amy and Jessica nodded.

"Well, I managed to tear everything out and put them back in right. But then . . ." Lila sighed. "Well, I was trying to add some material onto the hem because I'd made it a bit too short. And I made a terrible mistake."

Jessica hid a smile. "What happened?"

"I cut off the whole hem. So now it's about four inches shorter than it was supposed to be, instead of two inches longer. You should see this thing! It's like a micromini. I can't possibly wear it. I'm going to have to try to find something that looks like it and buy it, and just pray Elinore doesn't figure it out."

"That's really nice, Lila. You're going to deceive your own teacher," Jessica scoffed.

Lila's eyes flashed. "Yeah? Well, what are you making, Jessica? An electronic boy-finder?"

"You'll see what I'm making," Jessica said triumphantly. "But not till Friday. It's a giant secret."

"I can hardly wait," Lila muttered.

"Quit arguing, you guys, and let's figure out what we're going to get Olivia for her birthday," Amy said.

"I can only think of one thing she wants. And I don't think we can wrap Stuart Bachman in a box," Lila said lightly.

Jessica's eyebrows shot up. "Olivia? And Stuart Bachman?" She couldn't believe her ears.

"You mean you haven't heard? You must be the only person in the whole school." Lila laughed. "Caroline Pearce is taking painting, too, and you know how good she is at keeping secrets!"

All three girls cracked up at this. Caroline Pearce had a reputation as the school gossip. She was much better now than she used to be, but she still passed stories along from time to time.

"Caroline told me that Olivia is so obvious, it's sickening," Lila went on, lowering her voice. "Apparently she's done everything but throw herself at him right in public. Everyone in the whole school is talking about it."

Jessica shook her head. "Well, at least she's got good taste. Stuart *is* very cute," she mused. "But he's kind of on the old side. Is he interested in her?"

Lila shrugged. "Who knows? Caroline says they've done stuff together outside of school." She giggled. "Maybe he's just waiting till her birthday to make a real move."

"In which case, he's got two days to wait!" Amy laughed. Then she pointed at a gift shop just ahead. "Let's go in there and see what we can find. They usually have nice stuff."

Lila stopped short at McMahon's Sewing Supplies. "You guys go ahead. I need to stop in here and get some more thread and a new zipper." She sighed. "I don't know if there's much chance of resurrecting this disaster of a dress, but if there is, I know I'd better get to work on it right away!"

Ten minutes later Lila was paying for the purchases she had made in McMahon's when she heard a familiar voice behind her. It was Mrs. Egbert, Winston's mother, engrossed in conversation with a woman Lila didn't know. Lila had moved away from the cash register, and Mrs. Egbert hadn't seen her.

"Good heavens, I was as surprised as I could be when I heard the news!" Lila heard Mrs. Egbert exclaim. "But then, I had a hunch when Bert Wilkins moved that he'd be coming back before too long. And now it looks like he's got that promotion just about wrapped up."

Bert Wilkins—he was Todd Wilkins's father! Lila ducked behind a pile of material so Mrs. Egbert wouldn't see her. For a minute she didn't hear anything, and she was afraid the women had moved out of earshot.

Ordinarily Lila wouldn't have thought there was anything Mrs. Egbert could say that she would want to overhear. But if there was new gossip about the Wilkins family, Lila certainly wanted to be in on it.

Todd Wilkins had been Elizabeth Wakefield's

boyfriend for a long, long time. Then his father had received the news he was going to be transferred by his company to Burlington, Vermont.

The Egberts and the Wilkinses were close friends, and when Todd came back to visit Sweet Valley, he often stayed at the Egberts' house.

But Todd hadn't been back in a long time now, not since he and Elizabeth had decided to let their long-distance romance turn into a friendship. Since then, each of them had gotten involved with other people. Lila inched closer, trying to hear what else Mrs. Egbert had to say.

"Apparently the head office called him last week," Mrs. Egbert was confiding. "We didn't learn his decision until last night. But as far as I can tell, it looks like a sure thing. The Wilkinses are coming back to Sweet Valley!"

Lila froze. She couldn't believe what she had heard. Back to Sweet Valley? Todd Wilkins was moving back here for good?

She couldn't believe it. Grabbing her package, she dashed out of the store, barely able to hide her elation. This was by far the most exciting thing to have happened around this place in ages, she thought. And she was the very first one to know about it!

"What's wrong with you?" Jessica demanded impatiently when Lila hurried to join Amy and Jessica in the gift shop. She was out of breath, and her face was flushed. "You look like you just won first prize in the triathlon."

Lila shrugged mysteriously. "Let's just say I heard an interesting piece of news," she murmured.

"What is it?" Jessica and Amy demanded in unison.

Lila grinned. "I can't tell you yet," she said sweetly. "But I promise it's *very interesting*. Especially to you, Jess."

Jessica was fuming. She couldn't stand having someone keep a secret from her.

Lila knew that. And she was playing her cards carefully. Because Jessica had something she wanted—no, *needed*—very badly. And Lila knew the longer she held out and kept the secret from Jessica, the more valuable it would become!

Eleven

Thursday morning Lila put one last session in on her dress, using her study hall to try and patch the hem material back on. It was a disaster. Nothing could save the dress, she decided. She would just have to reason with Elinore and point out that she couldn't possibly be expected to wear a rag like this in public.

"The whole point of the workshop is to design and *wear* your dress," the teacher said unsympathetically after Lila told her what a mess her dress had turned into. "I'm sorry, Lila. But you shouldn't feel embarrassed. I'm sure a lot of students' projects haven't turned out exactly the way they planned."

Lila's face burned with humiliation. Exactly the way they planned was one thing. But this piece of patched-together cloth was another. She just couldn't wear it, and that was all there was to it.

Lila, her eyes stormy, was just coming out of the office where she had found Elinore Whitcomb when she caught sight of Jessica at her locker across the hall.

"Jess," she moaned, crossing the hall to join her, "you wouldn't believe the mess I'm in." In a matter of seconds she had spilled out the terrible story. "Until this morning I didn't really think she'd stick to this idea of making us wear whatever we made. What am I going to do?"

Jessica barely even tried to be sympathetic. "Why don't you borrow something from Anika?" she asked sweetly, twirling her combination. "Sorry, Lila, but I've got to rush off and help Randy—I mean, see if Randy can help me—I mean. . . ." She shook her head, confused, but Lila hadn't heard a word she'd said anyway. She was too absorbed in her own problems.

"Listen, Jess," she said suddenly, as if it had just occurred to her, "I've got it! Why don't you let me borrow your dress? I can just tell Elinore Whitcomb that I spent all night slaving and it came out perfectly after all. I know yours looks almost exactly like mine—or at least how mine was supposed to look."

Jessica opened her locker and scrutinized its contents. "Li, I don't think that would be very fair to everyone else. It sounds like cheating to me." Her eyes fixed innocently on her friend. "Would it be *honest*, Lila?"

"Who cares," Lila said impatiently. "Jess, I

just can't wear this thing tomorrow! I hang out of it, and it looks absolutely terrible!" Jessica didn't seem to be relenting.

"Sorry," Jessica said, slamming her locker shut. She appeared to be greatly enjoying Lila's discomfort.

I've got to get her to lend it to me, Lila thought desperately. *I've just got to.*

Then suddenly the conversation she had overheard the previous afternoon flashed into her head, and a devious smile crossed her face. "Fine," she said nonchalantly. "Then I guess I can't tell you the major news I happen to have overheard. Even though it *directly* concerns your family." And she flounced off down the hall, knowing Jessica wouldn't be able to bear the suspense.

For a minute Jessica didn't say anything. She just stared at Lila and shifted her books from one arm to the other. Finally she relented. "Oh, all right," she muttered. "I'll bring the stupid dress in for you tomorrow." Her eyes darkened. "Now tell me! What did you hear?"

Lila shook her head. "I can't tell you yet. Not till you've actually given me the dress."

"That isn't fair," Jessica said, nonplussed. "Come on, Lila. Don't you trust me? A deal's a deal."

Lila crossed her arms and frowned. "How can I trust you when you don't trust me to tell the truth about Anika Hunt and my father?"

Lila had a point, Jessica thought. "OK," she said slowly. "I'll bring the dress to school with me tomorrow morning. But does that mean I get to find out your secret the minute I hand it over?"

Lila nodded, her eyes shining. "That very minute," she crooned. "And not a minute before!"

"This is incredible!" Elizabeth gasped, grabbing Enid's arm. It was Friday afternoon, and the auditorium had been transformed. Each workshop had sectioned off a small area to display the final products. In the filmmaking area two TVs were running the videos the students had made. The pottery workshop had set up a miniature gallery to display their wares. Next to pottery was the engineering area, and beyond that, dress design, where students were modeling their dresses on a tiny ramp, like real models. Lila Fowler was listening with pleasure while everyone praised her dress. She felt especially triumphant because she had managed to get it from Jessica without giving away her secret about Todd Wilkins. There hadn't been time this morning because Jessica had arrived late with the dress. So Lila was enjoying her coup even more than she thought she would have. She knew Jessica would faint when she heard the news.

And Lila intended to wait for just the right moment to drop the bomb.

"It looks store bought!" Caroline Pearce gasped.

"Doesn't it?" Lila said proudly.

Beyond the dress design area were the paintings. Elizabeth had to admit that their work looked completely professional, set up on easels with little placards. Even her own painting, which she thought showed much more enthusiasm than talent, looked pretty.

"Wow," Enid said, moving forward for a closer look at Olivia's. "Yours turned out great!"

And it had. Olivia's painting, with its deep hues and abstract shapes, really stood out. "It should be hanging in a museum," Elizabeth said with admiration.

Each workshop split up so that some of its members were at their area to explain the work, while others could stroll around and see what their classmates had been doing for the past two weeks.

"I want to see what everyone thinks of Jessica's project," Elizabeth told Enid. "Come on, let's go back to the electronics area!"

To the girls' surprise, a group was clustered around Jessica's table. Jessica was sitting on one chair, while the chair beside her was reserved for her subjects. A large sign hanging over the table said Lie Detector. When Elizabeth and Enid pushed through to see what was going on, Jessica was about to demonstrate her device on her very first subject.

"Winston, let's do you first," she said.

Winston looked uneasily at the contraption. "I don't know if I like this," he said. "What if I have a lot to hide?"

Jessica grinned at him. "That's the whole point," she said, and everyone laughed.

Jessica's device, with Randy's help, had gotten considerably more sophisticated in the past day or two. Randy had linked the pulse detector to a computer and printer so that the lie detector's answer printed out almost immediately.

"Let's see," Jessica said, stroking her chin. "What should we ask Winston?"

"Ask him if he owes Matthews twenty-five dollars!" someone yelled from the back of the crowd.

Winston blushed deeply. He had made a bet with Ken Matthews the other week, had lost, and still hadn't paid up.

Winston stared at the device uneasily. "Jess, I don't like this thing," he muttered.

Jessica had already slid the pulse detector onto his finger and written down his pulse rate. "Go on," she commanded. "Do you owe Ken money?"

Winston blushed. "No," he said.

The printer hummed and whirred. Winston's normal pulse rate was compared to the current reading, and the detector's answer spat out of the small printer: "Lie!"

Everyone cheered riotously.

"Do someone else," Caroline Pearce begged.

"OK," Jessica said, pretending to be casual as she eyed the crowd. "How about, uh, Lila," she said, making an elaborate gesture of showing Lila to the chair.

Lila narrowed her eyes. "Don't make me confess about the dress," she hissed, sliding into the chair and allowing Jessica to hook her up to the machine.

"Step right up, folks! The great electronic lie detector will tell you all you want to know about your friends!" Jessica turned to Lila, crossing her arms sternly. "OK, here's the question. Is your father *really* going out with Anika Hunt?"

Lila stared at her, her brow furrowed. "What a dumb question. Of course he is," she said.

Jessica looked triumphantly at the printer, waiting for it to whir out the incriminating truth as the pulse detector picked up the real story. Sure enough, it whirred. It shot out the piece of paper with the answer: "Truth!"

The crowd roared. Jessica was dumbfounded. "Thanks for not giving away the dress thing," Lila whispered, sliding out of the chair. "You're a good friend, Jess."

Jessica barely knew what to do next. Truth? Lila's father really was going out with Anika?

Everyone was looking at her, and she had no

choice but to admit Lila had to be telling the truth after all. Either that, or admit her lie detector didn't work. And she didn't want to do that.

Caroline Pearce was pushing Olivia to the front of the crowd. "Olivia! Olivia!" a few girls started chanting.

All Jessica wanted to do was leave the auditorium. She felt completely gypped. The whole point of the lie detector was to expose Lila, make her look like a fool. She didn't care how great everyone else thought the device was. She felt completely let down.

In fact, she could barely muster up the enthusiasm to go through with Olivia's test.

"Ask her if she's in love with Stuart Bachman!" someone cried from the back of the crowd as Winston dragged Olivia toward the chair.

Olivia turned as red as a brick. "I'm not doing this thing," she cried, pulling free from Winston's grip. Before anyone else could touch her, she stormed off, her eyes spilling over with tears.

Elizabeth raced after her. "Olivia," she said, reaching out to touch her arm.

Olivia spun on her then. "How dare you, Elizabeth Wakefield! How dare you tell people that I'm in love with Stuart!"

Elizabeth stared at her. She couldn't believe her ears. Olivia almost never got angry. And what could she possibly mean about *her* telling people about Stuart?

"I never said a thing," Elizabeth told Olivia truthfully. "What are you talking about?"

"How do they all know, then?" Olivia cried. "You and Enid must have said something!"

"Olivia, I—"

But Olivia wouldn't let her finish. "What I feel about Stuart is my own business," she continued furiously. "I know you and Enid think he's too old for me and you don't approve for a million reasons. Well, you're not my mother, Elizabeth. You don't have any business judging me." She wiped tears from her eyes. "And you don't have any business telling other people about how I feel, either!"

Elizabeth stared at her friend in horror. But before she could say a word in her own defense, Olivia had stormed out of the auditorium.

"Uh-oh," Enid said, putting a soothing hand on Elizabeth's arm. "Looks like someone's just flipped out."

Elizabeth was so upset she could barely speak. "I don't know how Olivia thinks I could spread rumors about her. Doesn't she realize the whole school's been talking about the crush she has on Stuart?"

Enid shook her head. "She just needed someone to vent her anger on, Liz." She stared after Olivia. "I feel sorry for her. And it's her birthday, too."

Elizabeth drew in a long, shuddering breath. "I wonder if I should even go to her surprise party tonight," she whispered. "After what Olivia just said, I get the feeling I might not be very welcome."

"You're definitely coming," Enid said firmly. "Liz, whatever's going on with Olivia will sort itself out, and you two will make up. You know that."

Elizabeth didn't answer. She just hoped Enid was right.

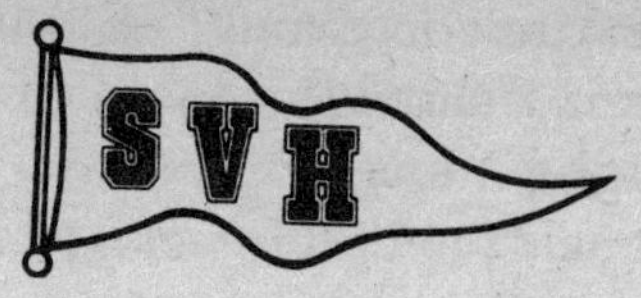

Twelve

It took Olivia almost an hour to calm herself down after the episode in the auditorium. She was so angry when she stormed out that she had to go outside and walk around the school. She didn't want to see a soul.

Then she began to feel uneasy about the scene she had made with Elizabeth. Elizabeth didn't seem like the sort of person who would spread rumors.

"I don't know what's wrong with me," Olivia said, sighing. She knew she ought to be thrilled that her painting had turned out as well as it had. And she should be enjoying her birthday and thinking about the evening to come. Instead, she had practically fallen apart the minute she knew that her classmates had found out how she felt about Stuart.

She tried to tell herself it didn't matter. After all, after today—and whatever surprise Stuart had in store for her—it would all come out in the open. She wouldn't have to feel embarrassed about liking him as much as she did. And everyone would see that he returned her feelings.

Thinking this way helped to calm Olivia down. By four-thirty, when she drove downtown to the gallery where Stuart's opening was being held, she actually felt pretty good. She had convinced herself that she had lost her temper in the auditorium because everyone else had been acting so childish. "I'm just much more mature than they are," she told herself. It would be such a relief to be at the opening with Stuart and his friends in the art world, where she knew she really belonged.

Olivia parked her van near the gallery, got out, and checked her reflection in a shop window. She had changed into her new jumpsuit in the girls' bathroom before she left school, and she had to admit she felt transformed—much more sophisticated than she usually did.

Olivia had never been to an opening before, and she didn't know what to expect. She was surprised, when she walked in, to see that no one was looking at the paintings, which had been carefully hung on the gallery walls. Everyone was standing around drinking white wine or seltzer water. The room was extremely crowded, and for a second Olivia panicked when she couldn't find Stuart.

"Wine or seltzer?" a waiter asked, coming by

with a silver platter. Olivia frowned at the tray. "Seltzer sounds good," she mumbled. She reached too quickly for the glass and spilled a little on her hand. She chided herself for her clumsiness. Everyone there must think she was about twelve.

Then she spotted Stuart, and everything was all right again. He was standing in one corner of the room, surrounded by people and talking animatedly. He looked fantastic. He had changed clothes, too, out of the jeans and sweater he'd been wearing at school and into a pair of pleated dark trousers and a dark houndstooth jacket. On someone else the clothes might have looked conservative, but not on him. To Olivia, he looked better than ever.

She took a tiny sip of seltzer and inched forward toward Stuart, trying to look as if she were used to this sort of thing. Just as she reached him a blond woman turned around and slipped her arm though Stuart's, then squeezed it lightly. "It's perfect," the woman said, giving him a huge smile.

Something about that smile made Olivia freeze in her tracks.

"Hi, Olivia," Stuart said, catching sight of her. "Come on over here! I've been telling everyone here about you. I want to show you off." He smiled at the blonde. "This is my prize student, the one I was telling you about."

Olivia inched forward, holding her glass and

trying not to stare at the woman. She wished she weren't wearing the idiotic jumpsuit. It seemed so self-consciously arty next to the blond's simple gray jersey dress.

"Olivia, this is Monica. Monica, Olivia," Stuart said.

Someone came up to congratulate Stuart then, and he turned away, leaving Olivia staring up at Monica, racking her brains for something to say. Monica was very tall and slender, so tall Olivia felt dwarfed beside her. She was extremely pretty with very classical features—gorgeous high cheekbones, creamy skin, and beautiful blue eyes. Her hair was cut in a simple blunt style with bangs. She appeared to be in her mid-twenties, and everything about her was composed and self-assured.

"Stuart's told me so much about your work," she said. Her voice had a slight accent to it, maybe British.

Olivia bit her lip. Who was this woman? She felt like crying.

"It's rare for him to lavish so much praise on a student. He thinks you'll go very far," Monica went on. She pushed her hair behind her ears, and Olivia froze when she saw her earrings—the ones that Stuart had designed!

Olivia gulped. Her first instinct was to flee. But she stayed rooted to the spot. Maybe Stuart and Monica were just friends. He had told her that he was planning a surprise for her—not for

Monica! She took a deep breath and was about to say something in response when another woman came up and kissed Monica on both cheeks, just the way they did in foreign movies.

"Monica! You look wonderful! Stuart's show is fabulous," the woman said, completely ignoring Olivia. "Darling, you must've been going nuts while he was putting it up. Did he even remember your birthday?"

Olivia blinked. She backed up, wanting nothing more than to escape. But there was no way to back off now without being obvious. Besides, Monica was turning toward her with that charming smile of hers. "Cyndi, this is Olivia, Stuart's star pupil. She helped Stuart choose the most fabulous present for me." She patted Olivia on the arm. "Did you know today is my birthday?"

This was too much. Olivia couldn't believe her ears at first. Monica's birthday—today?

"Uh, no, I didn't know," she blurted.

"Well, Stuart gave me that lovely frame, and he told me that you helped him choose it," Monica went on.

Olivia swallowed hard. She didn't think she could stand this for another minute. "Uh, excuse me, I-I want to look around at the paintings for a minute," she stammered, backing up and almost spilling her drink on a woman with bright turquoise hair.

She managed to get away just as Cyndi declared, "She's *adorable*. Stuart was so sweet to invite her!"

She makes it sound as though I'm in kindergarten, Olivia fumed, drawing away from the crowd and blinking back tears. The worst part was that Monica didn't even seem jealous of her! She acted completely and totally unthreatened.

But why should she be jealous when Olivia was only Stuart's star pupil, and Monica was clearly so much more?

There was no denying it. However much Olivia wanted to, she couldn't pretend that Monica and Stuart were just friends. Everything about them said otherwise. The way they looked at each other, the intimate smile Monica gave him when she touched his arm, the comfortable way Monica accepted the crowd's congratulations, as if she, as well as Stuart, had something to be proud of.

It was all too much. Olivia inched toward the door, sure she would be able to make a getaway without anyone noticing, when Stuart's glance fell on her.

"Olivia, where are you going?" he cried, loudly enough so that half the people in the room turned and stared.

Olivia blushed. "Uh, just to, uh . . ." She felt like a total moron.

"Don't you dare leave," Stuart commanded her with mock severity. "I have a special surprise for you. Remember?"

Olivia felt faint. She nodded dumbly, trying hard to keep a smile pasted on her face. The truth was, she wasn't sure at this point how many more surprises she could take.

"It's in the next room," Stuart said, taking her by the arm. He led her into a small room off the main gallery space where several smaller paintings were hanging. And right in the middle of the exhibit was Olivia's painting.

At first she couldn't believe her eyes. Right next to it was a small placard with her name on it.

Olivia was reeling. Her picture? Hanging up in here?

Once she had a chance to glance around she saw that there were several paintings, all by Riverside students hanging near hers. But Olivia's was right in the center. And it was the only one by a high school student.

"The gallery told me I could choose some student work to exhibit. And I especially wanted yours," Stuart said, beaming at her. "I managed to get it from school and bring it over in time without your knowing." He looked at her painting with delight.

Olivia was stunned. "You really think it's good enough to exhibit here? With your stuff?"

Stuart nodded. "I certainly do. In fact, several art critics have already commented on it. Your use of color and form, the texture you've managed to create. . . ." He studied her painting closely. "And now that your first work is being exhibited, the rest of the world will be able to see how good you are."

What Stuart was saying certainly seemed true. A number of people had crowded into the room where the student work was exhibited, and most of them seemed drawn to Olivia's painting. "This is remarkable!" she heard a man from the Riverside Academy exclaim, scrutinizing her work. "Stuart, where did you find this? It's a gem!"

"Isn't it breathtaking!" a woman standing near Monica said, looking right at Olivia's painting.

Olivia was overwhelmed with conflicting feelings. Her disappointment about Stuart and Monica was still sharp. But at the same time she was thrilled at seeing her work exhibited, and by the crowd's reaction to it.

"Stuart, thank you," she said in a low voice.

Suddenly she felt ashamed of herself. How could she have been so stupid? How had she become so obsessed with him as a potential boyfriend? Why hadn't she recognized that he had been an extraordinarily great teacher and a good friend? She had been acting like such a jerk, trying to make something romantic out of a teacher-student relationship. Yes, Stuart had been encouraging her. But not as a girlfriend, as a painter.

Everything suddenly became clear to Olivia. She realized how lucky she was to have Stuart's support—and his friendship. And when she realized how close she had come to blowing it all by doing or saying something inappropriate, she wanted to die!

"I want you to know, Olivia, what a genuine pleasure it's been to have you as a student. And I want you to promise to keep in touch," Stuart said seriously.

Olivia nodded. She wondered if Stuart knew she had had a crush on him, or if it even mattered.

But she decided, looking at her painting, that if he knew, he understood. More important, he respected her because she loved painting and because he thought she had talent. Having her painting in an exhibition was the very best birthday present she could possibly have been given.

On the way home Olivia decided to stop off at the Wakefields' house. She was tired, but she didn't think she would be able to relax until she had apologized to Elizabeth.

"Hi, Olivia!" Elizabeth said in surprise when she opened the front door. "Come on in."

"I can only stay a minute," Olivia said as she followed Elizabeth into the living room. Both girls sat down on the couch. "Oh, Liz, I'm so incredibly sorry about my outburst this afternoon," Olivia said in a rush. "I have no idea what got into me. I think I've just been a little out of it the past couple of weeks. Do you forgive me?"

"Of course," Elizabeth said, still surprised.

Olivia hung her head. "I made a fool out of myself over Stuart, didn't I?" she whispered.

"No, Olivia," Elizabeth said firmly. "You didn't. The fact is, you were the best student by far, and you had a right to get extra attention—and to demand it. I think you're going to be a great painter one day," she added.

Olivia shook her head. "Well, I don't know about that, but I learned a real lesson, Liz." Her eyes were very clear as she looked at her friend. "I think when we started these workshops two weeks ago I was so obsessed about not having a boyfriend that I just went crazy when I met Stuart. I wanted to be in love so badly. So when he encouraged me, when he tried to be a good teacher and help me, I took it all the wrong way." She sighed. "It isn't an easy lesson to learn. Today I found out the hard way that Stuart's feelings for me have nothing to do with anything but friendship. But I guess that's what really matters in the long run." She blinked back tears. "It hurts a lot right now, but I'll get over it. Anyway, thanks for being such a good friend, for putting up with me through all of this."

"Oh, Olivia," Elizabeth cried, throwing her arms around her and giving her a big hug. "Happy birthday!"

Olivia stared at her. "Boy, I almost forgot," she said slowly. "You know, today has been a really big day. But it doesn't feel like my birthday at all."

She was glad Elizabeth forgave her. But she couldn't help feeling wistful as she drove home. She was still thinking about Stuart and Monica and the special birthday celebration they would share.

Olivia knew it was going to be a long, long time before she forgot Stuart Bachman. In her heart she knew that things had been resolved the way they should be. But she would miss him nonetheless.

And she had to admit it hurt, going home alone with no special plans for her birthday that night. Not even the special knowledge of how well her painting had been received could make it any easier.

Thirteen

Olivia was exhausted by the time she got home. "I'm going upstairs to take a hot bath," she told her mother.

"Sweetheart, I need to ask you a big favor," her mother said. "I know you said you didn't want us to do anything special for your birthday, but I still thought you might like to go out to dinner with your dad and me. There's one problem, though. Your dad's car is in the shop, and he'll need to be picked up at the office at seven forty-five. I told him that you'd go get him. Is that OK?"

Olivia nodded. "That's fine," she said, glancing at her watch. "That still gives me time for a bath, though."

Her mother looked at her closely. "Do you feel all right, dear? You look a little pale."

Olivia smiled. "It's just been a long day, Mom.

One of those days when it seems as if you've grown up a whole year."

Her mother gave her an affectionate hug. "You're so young, sweetie. Your life is just beginning!"

Olivia hugged her mother back. "I know that, Mom. I really do."

She was so tired but strangely happy. Deep down she had to admit it was a relief that her crush on Stuart was over. She had been getting so worked up over him. And she was really happy her parents were taking her out for her birthday. And it was nice to have time just to relax. In fact, she ended up dawdling in a bubble bath for so long that she had to hurry to meet her father by seven forty-five.

They drove back home together, talking animatedly about Olivia's painting. "I really want you to see the exhibition, Daddy," she was saying when she opened the door to the house.

The hallway was dark.

"Mom?" Olivia called, stepping forward and groping for the light.

The next minute dozens of voices screamed, "SURPRISE!"

Olivia thought she was going to fall down. She gasped and grabbed onto her father's arm, staring in disbelief as lights came on and her friends jumped up from behind the sofas in the living room, from out of closets, everywhere imaginable.

"Were you surprised? Really surprised?" Enid Rollins asked anxiously.

Olivia was so shocked she could barely speak.

"I think that means yes," Elizabeth said, giggling.

For the next few minutes pandemonium was the rule. Everyone was crowding around Olivia, hugging her, wishing her a happy birthday. Winston hurried over to put music on the stereo, and Mrs. Davidson brought out a huge pile of presents. Olivia felt absolutely overwhelmed. Everyone—all her friends—had made it. Then her gaze fell on Stuart and Monica.

"What are you doing here?" she demanded. "Monica, I thought today was your birthday, too!"

"It is," Monica admitted. "But Stuart and I decided to wait and celebrate it tomorrow night." She gave Olivia a big smile. "He really didn't want to miss this."

"You're not kidding I didn't," Stuart said, giving Olivia a hug.

Olivia squeezed her eyes shut. She had thought so often about what it would be like to be hugged by Stuart. She blinked to hold back tears. What an incredible day!

"I can't believe this," she said, backing up to look around the living room. In the half hour she had been gone, it had been transformed. Balloons and streamers hung everywhere, vases of fresh flowers sat on every table, and everyone she knew from school was there, beaming at her as her mother brought in a cake covered with candles.

Rod Sullivan was standing right next to her. "Hi," he said in a shy voice, handing her a beautifully wrapped package. "This is for you, Olivia."

Olivia met his smile. Rod looked so nice tonight. And the expression on his face made her want to give him another chance. Who knew what might happen?

Everything felt so magical right at that moment, it seemed as if anything were possible. Olivia really meant it when she told Rod how glad she was that he was there.

She felt sure she was going to cry when everyone started singing happy birthday. She couldn't get over how lucky she was. It was the best birthday of her entire life.

"I can't believe you brought that thing here," Lila complained when Jessica started fooling around with her lie detector halfway through Olivia's party.

"Why?" Jessica narrowed her eyes. She was too excited over the success of her lie detector to leave it at home, especially since, detached from the printer, it was perfectly portable. "Do you have something to hide, Lila? You know, sometimes it doesn't work right the first time. Let me try it on you again."

"Look," Lila said, sighing, "I don't care what you do to me, Jess. The fact is, Daddy and Anika *are* going out. And if you still don't believe me, just wait till the next issue of *Celebrity* magazine comes out. They're going to be on the cover, along with six other couples. They're doing a feature on the private lives of Hollywood starlets."

Jessica groaned. "All right, I give in," she muttered. "I guess you really were telling the truth. But speaking of telling the truth," she added, "you still haven't paid up, Lila. You still haven't told me the big secret that got you my dress today."

Ken Matthews and Aaron Dallas had come over to inspect Jessica's lie detector when she started fooling around with it. "Jessica, I'm impressed," Ken said, admiring the way it was put together. Jessica glanced at Lila with annoyance. Yet another chance for her to hang on to her secret even longer.

"Thanks. Mr. Drexel liked it, too," Jessica said.

"Did you actually make it yourself?" Ken continued, staring at it.

Jessica fidgeted a little. "Of course," she said finally, now that several of her classmates had joined them to hear what was going on. Randy Mason was within earshot, but Jessica knew she could count on him to keep their secret. She gave him a smile, and he looked away, blushing.

"I don't believe it," Lila declared. "Jess,

put your finger in this thing and let's test you!"

Everyone cheered, and Jessica turned bright red.

"I don't think that's necessary," she said haughtily, trying to wriggle free. But it was too late. Ken and Lila forced her finger into the contraption.

"How do you tell if it's a lie or not?" Ken demanded.

Randy cleared his throat. "It's been dismantled from its printing device, so you'll have to rely on the pulse gauge." He coughed. "First, you establish Jessica's resting pulse rate. Then ask her a question. If her pulse speeds up, she's lying. Otherwise, she's telling the truth."

Ken noted that Jessica's pulse rate was seventy-two.

"Jessica," Lila said solemnly, "did you really and truly make this lie detector yourself?"

"Of course," Jessica said again, trying to breathe slowly and calmly so her pulse wouldn't change.

"Look, it's speeding up!" Ken cried, looking at the gauge.

Jessica bit her lip. "Stupid thing," she scoffed. "You can't expect it to work all the time." She couldn't stand having everyone laughing at her. "All right," she cried, looking straight at her sister. "How about you, Liz. You haven't tried this thing yet."

Elizabeth looked surprised. "Sure," she said coming forward.

Jessica didn't really have a question to ask her sister. All she cared about right then was shifting attention away from herself, even if it meant putting her twin on the spot.

By now almost a dozen people had come over to see what was going on. Jessica strapped her sister's finger into the lie detector and deliberated over what to ask her.

But she couldn't think of a thing.

Then Lila came forward, a sly smile on her face. "I have a question for Liz," she said. "That is, if you can't think of one, Jess." She gave Jessica a triumphant smile. "I guess my secret won't be a secret much longer," she whispered.

Jessica stared at her, confused. The crowd kept their eyes on Lila, waiting to hear her question.

Lila put her hands on her hips. "I happen to know for a fact that Todd Wilkins is moving back to Sweet Valley. Now, tell the truth, Liz. Are you the slightest bit concerned about the reappearance of your old boyfriend? Or are things going to stay the same between you and Jeffrey?"

Dead silence fell over the crowd. For a minute no one spoke. Then Winston cried. "How did you find out? It's supposed to be a secret! No one's supposed to know till next week, after they sell their house in Vermont!"

Jessica looked with horror at Lila. That was the secret Lila owed her? And Lila had somehow managed to keep it to herself until this very minute! It was lucky that Jeffrey hadn't been able to come to the party. At least he didn't have to hear the news this way.

Elizabeth sat perfectly still, her face pale. Without saying a word she slid her finger out of Jessica's lie detector. "I don't think I need this thing," she said calmly. But the cloudy expression in her eyes contradicted the evenness of her voice. She got up without saying a word and left the room.

What will happen to Elizabeth and Jeffrey when Todd Wilkins returns to Sweet Valley? Find out in Sweet Valley High #58, **BROKENHEARTED.**

NOW
SWEET VALLEY HIGH®
IS A GAME!

- RACE THROUGH THE HALLS OF SWEET VALLEY HIGH
- MEET SWEET VALLEY'S MOST POPULAR GUYS
- GO ON 4 SUPER DREAM DATES

You and your friends are students at Sweet Valley High! You can be Jessica, Elizabeth, Lila or Enid and go on a dream date. Live the excitement of the Junior Prom, or go to a Sweet Sixteen Party. You can go surfing or join the bike tour. Whatever you choose, be sure to watch out for the other girls. To keep you from winning, they might even steal your boyfriend.

YOU'LL FIND THIS GREAT MILTON BRADLEY GAME AT TOY STORES AND BOOK STORES NEAR YOU!

- ☐ 27416 SLAM BOOK FEVER #48 $2.95
- ☐ 27477 PLAYING FOR KEEPS #49 $2.95
- ☐ 27596 OUT OF REACH #50 $2.95
- ☐ 27650 AGAINST THE ODDS #51 $2.95
- ☐ 27720 WHITE LIES #52 $2.95
- ☐ 27771 SECOND CHANCE #53 $2.95
- ☐ 27856 TWO BOY WEEKEND #54 $2.95
- ☐ 27915 PERFECT SHOT #55 $2.95
- ☐ 27970 SHIPWRECKED! #56 $2.95

Prices and availability subject to change without notice

Buy them at your local bookstore or use this page to order.

- -

Bantam Books, Dept. SVH7, 414 East Golf Road, Des Plaines, IL 60016

Please send me the books I have checked above. I am enclosing $______ (please add $2.00 to cover postage and handling). Send check or money order—no cash or C.O.D.s please.

Mr/Ms ____________________

Address ____________________

City/State ________________ Zip ________

SVH7—6/89

Please allow four to six weeks for delivery. This offer expires 12/89.

MURDER AND MYSTERY STRIKES

America's favorite teen series has a hot new line of

Super Thrillers!

It's super excitement, super suspense, and super thrills as Jessica and Elizabeth Wakefield put on their detective caps in the new SWEET VALLEY HIGH SUPER THRILLERS! Follow these two sleuths as they witness a murder . . . find themselves running from the mob . . . and uncover the dark secrets of a mysterious woman. SWEET VALLEY HIGH SUPER THRILLERS are guaranteed to keep you on the edge of your seat!

YOU'LL WANT TO READ THEM ALL!

☐	#1: DOUBLE JEOPARDY	26905-4/$2.95
☐	#2: ON THE RUN	27230-6/$2.95
☐	#3: NO PLACE TO HIDE	27554-2/$2.95
☐	#4: DEADLY SUMMER	28010-4/$2.95

Bantam Books, Dept. SVH5, 414 East Golf Road, Des Plaines, IL 60016

Please send me the books I have checked above. I am enclosing $______ (please add $2.00 to cover postage and handling). Send check or money order—no cash or C.O.D.s please.

Mr/Ms ____________________

Address ____________________

City/State ____________________ Zip ________

SVH5—7/89

Please allow four to six weeks for delivery. This offer expires 1/90.